A SC...
REVELATION

Sally clutched Will's arm. "Will, where is all this leading?"

He frowned. "I'm not entirely sure, but I don't much like it!"

"Alex has done something very wrong. That's what you think, isn't it?"

"That's what I suspect," Will said quietly.

"I can't believe it! I don't want to believe it! I think you're just jealous! You and your friends never did like Alex."

"Ah, here you are, Sally. I hope you recall you have promised the next waltz to me!"

Sally turned to see Alex standing behind her, smiling. With shaking hands, she withdrew the engagement ring from her finger and gave it to Will.

"I don't think I will need this anymore, thank you," she said coldly.

Will, his expression impassive, gave her a short bow. "Just as you wish."

By Rebecca Baldwin

A LADY OF FASHION

A TANGLED WEB

Available from HarperPaperbacks

A TANGLED WEB

Rebecca Baldwin

HarperPaperbacks
A Division of HarperCollinsPublishers

This is a work of fiction. The characters, incidents, and
dialogues are products of the author's imagination and are not
to be construed as real. Any resemblance to actual events or
persons, living or dead, is entirely coincidental.

 HarperPaperbacks   *A Division of* HarperCollins*Publishers*
                                10 East 53rd Street, New York, N.Y. 10022

Cover illustration by Ted Sizemore

First printing: February 1995

Printed in the United States of America

HarperPaperbacks, HarperMonogram, and colophon are
trademarks of HarperCollins*Publishers*

❖ 10 9 8 7 6 5 4 3 2 1

London
2 September

My Dearest Sally—

I received your last letter, dear sister, and sympathize entirely with your feelings on putting off black gloves at last!!!! As unseemly as it may seem to others, particularly Mama and Papa, to feel relieved by the end of the mourning period for Great Aunt Sarah, you will understand when I say that it was particularly disobliging of her to go off right in the middle of your first London Season! Of course, Great Aunt Sarah was an extremely disobliging old lady, so you may guess at my surprise and happiness for you when you wrote that she had remembered her namesake (you!!!!) with such a handsome bequest! Fifty thousand pounds is a handsome fortune, Tilghman says, and I must agree with Mama that it comes as shock since G.A.S. never paid the least attention to any of us when she was alive. I know I am wicked for saying these things, but you know it is true! Oh, Sally, I do miss the days when we shared a room and all our confidences. I wish you were here now! Wait! I have an idea!!!!!

Since Tilghman is always so busy these days with his work, whatever it is, in the Foreign Office, and town is somewhat thin of company right now, I have had some time to think, and I have come up with what I think is a wonderful plan! Come for the Little Season! Now that I have been a married woman for quite a year or more, Mama need not come to London with you, since I have been on the town long enough to be quite able to chaperone you about in a most respectable fashion. I know that Mama was quite fagged to death last year between my wedding and your debut, and she hates town's hustle and bustle anyway, so this would be a perfect solution, rather than waiting for next year. Besides, I should like it very much if you were here to bear me company, for Tilghman works so hard, and is so preoccupied that I rarely see him. Everyone said when we were engaged, that I was making a Good Match, that Lord Tilghman would go far in the Foreign Office, but no one explained to me how hard he would work!

Nonetheless, there is much to keep us busy, and now that we are out of mourning, we can do as much as we like! I daresay you would not know me now, for I have become quite a lady of fashion and like the way of a married lady much better than that of a debutante! Now that we're out of mourning, I go racketing about town all the time and occupy my time with all manner of fashionable activities, parties, etc., etc. I daresay that Papa would be just a little shocked at some of the tonnish pleasures we enjoy, but everyone does it, so there cannot be any harm in it, no matter what Tilghman might say.

Later.

    My dearest Sally, you will never, ever guess in a million years who has just come to call and sat for upward of half an hour in the drawing room, as big as life and more handsome than ever! ALEX QUARTERMAINE !!!!!!!!!!!!!!!????!!!!!!! Can you believe it? I swear, I am ready to faint from shock! I am not quite certain what happened that he had to leave town so suddenly last Season, but he seems none the worse for it and asked quite civilly after you! When I said that I hoped that you would be in Town soon to be bear me company through the Little Season, he said that he hoped he would see you at Almack's, so you may be sure that he is still good ton. Only fancy, he has asked me to a card party at Duchess of D.'s tonight. I think I shall go!

    I've written a separate letter to Mama and Papa asking them to let you come to me. I'm sorry this letter is so long, but I am sure that Tilghman will frank it for me. I must close now as I must get ready to attend this card party tonight with Alex!

I am,
Your Affectionate Sister,
Julia

P.S. The state drawing room is done. I decided on the regal crimson damask after all. The house is still in an uproar of workmen, however.

2

Heat lay heavily across the late August landscape.

William Starret, carrying his rod and creel basket, walked up the hill from the river. No London valet would have countenanced his boots, sadly scuffed and water-stained, nor would a proper gentleman's gentleman have allowed his master to appear in public in an open-necked shirt without collar or cravat, with his nut brown locks wildly curling beneath a battered felt hat stuck with fishing flies. In deference to the late summer heat, he wore his nankeen jacket tied around his waist, a solecism that would have placed him beyond the pale in fashionable circles. In short, he looked like a man who had been fishing and had enjoyed himself enormously at the sport.

His spaniels were frisking around his feet, but at the sight of the young lady seated on the low wall of the churchyard, they yelped joyfully and tore off in her direction. They romped about her skirts, uttering happy barks of pleasure.

"Daisy! Sport!" Will cried, but the dogs paid little attention, enthusiastically greeting a favorite human who could be trusted to pet them and play their favorite game.

Miss Sarah Blythe, in a light sprig muslin round gown and a wide-brimmed chipstraw hat, gently disengaged the canines' muddy paws from her skirts and uttered the magic word *"stick!"* that sent them off in search of something she could throw for them, a diversion of which they never seemed to tire.

Without preamble, Will sank down on the low stone wall beside Sally, blotting at his brow with a spotted kerchief. "Hot enough for you?" he asked. "Lord, I've never seen an August this hot!"

Rather than taking exception to his casual dress and decidedly fishy aura, which many another lady might have done, Sally merely handed him the crossed and folded epistle she had been carrying in one hand. "Just look what Julia has to say!" she announced, and leaned back against the cool stone to wait his reaction, fanning herself with her furled parasol.

"It's too hot to decipher your sister's handwriting," Will said mildly, but he took the letter anyway.

Will and Sally, having played together since childhood, knew each other as well as two people could, and there was no need for either of them to stand upon ceremony. Will crossed his legs and made himself comfortable in the shade, fanning himself with his hat.

He was a pleasant-looking man, just a shade past his twenty-second birthday, with a stocky build and an open face distinguished by a ready smile and eyes his mother frequently called "an honest blue." Everything he was thinking was writ plain in his expression. As he scanned the letter, his eyes flickered beneath his lashes.

Sally, who was perfectly used to his expressions, paid them little heed. Rather, she twirled her little parasol impatiently, waiting for him to finish. When Sport and Daisy returned, lugging a rather rotted branch, she played with them absently, her features set in a rather pensive expression.

Although Julia was the Beauty of the family, Sally had a winsome appeal. Nearly as tall as her companion, at nineteen, she was made along strong lines, with a heart-shaped face and a pair of speaking brown eyes set beneath dark brows. While some might deplore her red hair, it was a warm copper shade, thick and lustrous, which put her a little out of the ordinary. A tendency to freckle, much worried over by her mama, caused her to venture out, under strict orders, only beneath a wide-brimmed hat and the aforementioned sunshade.

Since, in her mother's day, ladies never ventured beyond their father's gardens without, at the very least, a footman in attendance, she might have considered herself fortunate that she was not saddled with one or the other of her younger siblings, especially since she had some things to discuss with Will that were extremely private. As it was, she had been obliged to take a rather circuitous route along the hedgerows that marked the border between her father's property and that of the Starrets's, lest she be seen by prying eyes. There was, she knew, no privacy in a country neighborhood.

It had been her intention to waylay Will in some place where their conversation could not be overheard. When her father said Will was trying his hand with some new flies, she knew precisely where to find him. Since she knew his habits as well as he, her wait was not long. Had her thoughts not been agitated by the letter she had received, she might have enjoyed a solitary sojourn at the edge of the ancient churchyard. Churchyards were just then considered very romantical places by her peers, perfect places to brood over lost loves and unrequited emotions. Since her debut the previous year, Sally had been prone to consider herself not only very fashionable but also far more worldly than actuality might have indicated. That Will never hesitated to puncture her new found pretension to sophistication never failed to annoy her. However, he had been on the town a few years so she had to defer to his experience, if only grudgingly. Still, she had decided Will was completely devoid of any sort of romantic sensibility whatsoever.

Unlike Alex Quartermaine.

Before she could immerse herself in pleasant fantasies about Alex, one of her favorite leisure activities, Will had folded the letter up and handed it back to her.

"Very nice for you!" he said mildly. "Alex Quartermaine is back in town, and it sounds as if Julia is as fashionable as a five pence!" He looked at her. "Now, what's the problem, Sally? And don't roundabout with me, because there's no earthly reason for you to want me to read Julia's letter if you didn't want something."

While she had been waiting for him, she had rehearsed her speech carefully, but now that Will was here, stolid and phlegmatic, she gave in to impulse. "I do have a *little* idea, and I need your help," she admitted.

Will stood up, shaking his head. His expression took on a mulish cast. "Oh, no, you don't do that!" he said. "Told you the last time you had one of your *little ideas* that I wasn't getting involved in it! Remember the drawing-room curtains, and the ghost, and the time I got sent down from Oxford? Oh, no! Up to snuff now, you know! Not about to get involved in one of your harebrained schemes, my girl!"

Whenever Will was extremely upset, he tended to blush. His face at that moment was taking a pinkish hue.

Sally picked up the stick proffered by Daisy and threw it across the path into a meadow. The dogs bounded after it, oblivious. "Those," she said grandly, "were things we did when we were children, Will! And besides, it was your sister Louisa and my sister Julia who set the drawing-room curtains on fire! I was nowhere around!"

"Just the same, you have a knack for harebrained schemes, Sally, admit you do! Julia and Louisa were in hysterics over that ghost trick you played! Governess quit over that, too! Which wasn't such a bad thing, because she was very bad to m'sisters, always thrashing and threatening them! But that don't signify now! Besides, you're the one who's always prosing on how you're beyond all of that now that you're on the marriage market!"

"If you mean now that I have made my debut, yes, I am much more mature and worldly now!" Sally replied loftily, stung by his vulgar description. "And now that I have a little town bronze, I am much more up to every rig and row in town!"

Will hooted. He pitched the stick the two dogs were eagerly offering him; Daisy and Sport tore over the wall into the churchyard. "Well, at least that inheritance ought to make Alex Quartermaine come up to snuff at last!" he added with the brutal honesty only a very close friend can deliver.

Sally's eyes grew huge and two bright spots of color appeared on her cheeks. She put her tongue between her teeth and made a hissing sound, standing up and moving toward Will in a threatening manner.

"Odious!" she said. "And all because he beat you out with that lady bird from Covent Garden you both fancied so much!"

"I say, Sal! Doing it too brown, besides, ladies aren't supposed to know about things like that!"

"Well, you told me about it, and besides, they do!" Sally retorted. "Anyway, that doesn't have anything to do with it—I am sure that Alex is above such vulgar considerations as money."

Suddenly, Will stopped and looked around. A

thin, weedy man in clerical garb was coming from the Rectory. "Oh, damme!" he said.

"Here comes the vicar, and ten to one he will want to go on about Sport and Daisy playing in the churchyard and what damage they do, which isn't true at all!"

Without another word, Will and Sally took discreet flight, losing themselves in the copse of beeches as they headed down toward the river, behaving more like the naughty children they were than the mature, sophisticated adults they believed themselves to have become.

They headed automatically for a shady green bank hidden by a stand of willows and threw themselves into the grass, where they covered their mouths, vainly trying to muffle their laughter. This had been the refuge of their childhood, and it remained a refuge today.

"Did you see the look on his face? Oh, lord!" Sally giggled.

"Exactly," said Will. He rolled over on his back and stared up at the sky through the rustling green fronds. It was cooler here than anywhere else. "Doubtless, he will report all to the Vestry Committee, and my father will feel obligated to give me a lecture." Will sighed. "Lately, it seems as if all we do is go around. Fa feels that I should settle down and take my responsibilities seriously. He keeps saying he's not getting any younger, and that I ought to be doing more about managing the estate. And I quite agree with him, but it seems as if every time I do try to take up the reins, it's not to his satisfaction! Even Helmsley, our bailiff, says I am doing very well. And I ought to, you know, for I was bred to the job! But I would rather do anything than fight with Fa, for you know what he's like when his gout's upon him!"

"Exactly so," Sally replied. Sincerely fond of Sir Walton and Lady Starret, she still had to admit that Will's papa could be sadly unreasonable, especially with his only son, when his painful disorder was afflicting him. "And I am very glad you brought that up, for I think that I might have a solution that would suit you very well!"

"Oh, no! Told you before, Sally, none of your schemes!" Will said, looking at her uneasily.

"But this is so very satisfactory, and such a grand idea!" Sally replied eagerly. "Will, would you be so very good as to become engaged to me?"

He sat straight up. "WHAT?" Will asked in an awful voice.

Sally took a deep breath. "I said, 'Will, would you be so very good as to become engaged to me?'" she repeated matter-of-factly.

For a moment, Will was nonplussed. Then he began to laugh.

In all her calculations, this was the only reaction Sally had not anticipated. "Well, it wasn't that ludicrous an idea," she said, deeply stung. "Lots of men would like to marry me, I daresay. Why, I turned down two *very* respectable offers last year!"

Will could not find his voice for laughter. He whooped and shook his head, holding his midsection. He pounded his fist against his thigh and chortled.

"Marry you?" he asked, going off again. "That's a good one, Sally!"

"I didn't say you had to marry me, you idiot!" Sally cried, deeply offended. "I just asked you if you would become *engaged* to me!"

"It's six of one, a half dozen of the other," Jack replied. "And it won't do, Sally! For one thing, we ain't in love, and for another you're mad for Alex—" Enlightenment dawned. "Ah, now I see how it is! You think if I offer for you, it will make Alex jealous enough to finally come up to snuff!"

Sally, torn between annoyance and a desire to convince Will to see things her way, twisted fretfully. "Well, I have been giving it a great deal of thought, and I am convinced that it will work. Besides which, it will make your father happy and convince him that you are accepting your responsibilities. After all, your parents and my parents have always hoped we would make a match of it—"

"Which was precisely why we determined that we would never do so!" Will put in.

"Yes, but we were just children then! Anyway, if you would just listen to me, Will, I will show you how it would work for you, too!"

Will shook his head. "Oh, I'm all ears," he promised. He looked toward Sally with such an expression of mock seriousness that she had to laugh in spite of herself.

"I know this sounds dreadful. Oh, Will, I had really thought about it and rehearsed what I would say so very carefully, and now I have made a sad botch of it. But we would both get what we want, you see!"

Will broke off a tuft of grass and chewed on it thoughtfully. "Sounds to me as if you have too much time on your hands," he said with total candor.

"Well, I wouldn't, if I were to go to London, you know! And neither would you!"

"Oh, I'm going to town, never fear! With the harvest coming on and m'father in his present mood, best to be far out of reach! Let him see then how he goes on! That should prove to him that I am capable of running things very well, thank you!" Will frowned. "You'd think I'd never stacked a rick or run a crew of threshers! Acts as if I were born and bred in London. Me, what's been farming since I was old enough to drive a team! Besides, I have another interest in Miss Quinn. A beauty she is, too! That's who *I* shall be looking for when I go up to town!"

"Miss Quinn? The actress who plays all the breeches parts? Will, is *she* your high flyer?"

Will looked down at Sally, bemused. Clearly she, at least, was not as sophisticated as she thought.

"She's my interest, yes! But *you* don't know anything about that!" Will warned her sternly. "Ladies don't!"

"I won't breathe a word," Sally promised. "But she is very pretty, and *that* is a very good reason to go to London!"

"I think so," Will smiled. "And a very good reason not to be stuck at Almack's every night! Lots of other fellows out there interested in her too, you know."

But, Sally noted, at least he had not said no . . . yet. A good sign. From somewhere, the spaniels appeared, dashing past them and plunging into the water where they frolicked about before returning to shore to share their wet coats and muddy paws with their human companions.

She plunged ahead. "Don't you think it would make your father happy if you were to announce your engagement to me? That would be a definite sign that you were settling down and taking your part in the estate seriously. And it would also give you a very good excuse to go up to town."

"What's that?" Will asked curiously.

"Wedding clothes and parties and preparations," Sally said vaguely. "One last fling before you settle down and all of that. Then, while you are gone, Sir Walton will see how very much he misses you when you are not there to do all the things that need to be done. All our friends will be waiting to congratulate us, don't you think?"

"I don't think, and I think it's a damned shabby trick to play on them, and on your parents and mine!" Will said baldly. "Besides, what makes you think Alex will come up to scratch? He had most of an entire Season last year, and for all I could see, all he did was flirt! Sally, you've had some stupid ideas in your time, but this is about the worst. Even for you, it's a stupid idea, and you must admit you've had some corkers before!"

Sally sat straight up. She pulled her skirt, now sadly smeared with dog's paw prints, down over her knees and looked loftily down her nose at him. "Will, if I didn't have to be nice to you right now, I would cheerfully drown you!" she exclaimed.

It was Will's turn to sit up. "Listen, Sally," he laid a hand on her arm, his tone serious. "Not at all sure that I like Alex Quartermaine anyway! Only met him once or twice, but you get a feeling about people. Thing of it is, Sally, you could do a lot better! Alex ain't all the thing."

"Oh, pooh! Besides, Alex is very good ton! Julia says so!"

"Julia's not as up to snuff as she thinks," Will replied darkly. He searched about for words to describe his feelings. "Most men don't like him as a matter of fact! Ask anyone! Ask Frank! Ask Barney! Not a nice fellow, Alex. Daresay Tilghman don't care for him, either!"

Having had a year to contemplate the virtues of the absent Mr. Quartermaine, Sally was not to be discouraged. "You're just jealous! You and Frank and Barney, all jealous! None of you could hold a candle to Alex! He's handsome and polished and charming."

Will had to admit that this description of Alex Quartermaine was accurate, to the best of his knowledge. He was not surprised that Sally would dismiss himself, Frank Holmes, and Barney Tennant as having opinions of no account, let alone being without looks, charm or address to equal Mr. Quartermaine's. It is very hard to feel romantic toward young men who have been known to you all your life. However, he did feel that their opinions might bear some weight for the same reason and said so.

"That's because none of you understand Alex as I do," Sally said hotly. "If you but knew him better, you would understand how deep and soulful he really is. He only needs to be loved, you see!"

Will snorted. "Sounds like a bag of moonshine to me," he sneered, shaking his head. "Been reading novels again, haven't you? Too much time on your hands entirely."

"I wouldn't expect you to understand," Sally responded. "You don't know Alex like I do! Besides, I am sure he would have proposed had I not been called out of town when Great Aunt Sarah died."

"So you think if you and I pretend to be engaged, he'll get jealous and come up to snuff?" Will asked.

"Well, something like that," Sally admitted. "Don't you see? If Alex thinks that I am engaged to marry another, it will awaken him to his true feelings."

"Sounds like great deal of nonsense to me, Sally. Alex ain't likely to cut in on another man's territory! Dashed bad ton, you know!"

"But I love him!" Sally spoke the words that have led women to disaster since the world began. "Don't you see, Will, when he sees that I am engaged to another, he will *have* to declare himself!"

Will groaned. "It won't work, Sally. Take my word for it, I know. And then where will we be? There won't be anything for it but for us to get buckled!"

It had not occurred to Sally that Alex would not offer for her. She could imagine no other fate than to be married to him. "He will," she told Will fiercely. "I know he will!"

"How do you know that? You haven't heard a

word from him since you left town last year. You'd think if the fella cared for you, he'd have written or visited by now!"

"Julia says he has been out of town."

"Sounds like he had to rusticate for a while. And that is *not* a good sign." Will chewed on his grass thoughtfully. "Anyway, what's to say that he wouldn't offer for you just to get his hands on your inheritance?"

"Alex would never do that," Sally replied serenely.

It was on the tip of Will's tongue to say something else equally cutting, but at that moment, one large, perfect tear rolled down Sally's cheek.

"I love him so much, Will. I'll *die* if I can't have him. Besides," she added, "Mama and Papa would be very likely not to allow me to go to town and stay with Julia without Mama if they knew! They would say Julia isn't steady enough to chaperone me! If I'm engaged to you, they'll certainly let me go! And I do so want to go to London!"

"No need to make a watering pot of yourself!" Will cried uneasily. "Damme it, Sally, that dog won't hunt!"

Nonetheless, a second tear rolled down Sally's cheek.

There was nothing that could have made Will feel more helpless than the sight of a woman crying.

"Damme it, Sally, stop that!" he faltered. "Not the all thing at all!"

"I daresay I shall be all right in a moment," Sally replied, focusing upon some distant point. "Oh, I *never* cry! This is so stupid!" She rooted in a pocket. "And I don't have a handkerchief, either! Stupid! Stupid, stupid, *stupid*!"

Wordlessly, Will handed her his own and she used it to dab at her eyes and blow her nose.

After a moment, during which he waved away the handkerchief as she tried to return it to him, Will swallowed and said thoughtfully, "You really do love this fella, don't you?"

Sally nodded, blowing her nose again. She did not look her best in tears.

"Well, what if he don't come up to snuff after all of this?" Will asked.

"He will. He will! I know he will!" Sally promised wildly. "You see, he will only need a little push! He was almost on the verge when I left town, you see. Oh, Will, I promise, if he doesn't, I'll cry off and you'll be safe! Everyone will be angry with me, not you!"

Will swallowed hard. "All right, I'll do it!" he said. "But mind, I don't want to be dragged to Almack's every night! I have my own interests to pursue, you know!"

In response, Sally threw her arms around his neck. She kissed his cheek. Will put his arm affectionately around her shoulders and gave her a sporting hug. "I daresay I shall get used to the idea after a while," he said. "But mind, if he don't propose by the end of the Season, you're crying off!"

"I promise!" Sally agreed recklessly. "Oh, Will you are the best friend a girl ever had!"

Will laughed. "Tell that to Miss Quinn!"

• • •

"Well, my dear, young Starret has offered for our daughter's hand!" Mr. Blythe, emerging from the study, looked over his spectacles at his wife. His eyebrows were all the way up to the place where his hairline used to be, and he looked decidedly cynical about this endeavor. Will, following behind him, did not see his expression, but had a fairly good idea that Mr. Blythe suspected his middle daughter was up to her usual antics, but was determined to give the happy pair the benefit of the doubt.

Mrs. Blythe, engaged at that moment with darning some of her oldest son's stockings, received this news with a smile as she rose from her seat by the morning room windows. "Isn't this wonderful!" she said. "Will is such a nice boy. Welcome to the family, dear," she said, as Will bowed to receive a maternal peck on his forehead. "Sally said something about it this morning at breakfast, but I never know with her if she's serious or not." The experience of raising five lively offspring had completely removed surprise from her emotional vocabulary. Besides, this was not an unexpected event. "I should call her down so that we may all have a glass of Madeira together. Would you like to stay to dinner, dear?"

"You won't have to call her down, Mama," said Master Robert Blythe, who had been looking about in a closet for his cricket gear. "She's been sitting on the upstairs landing eavesdropping since Will rode up!"

"Rude, odious tattletale!" Sally herself emerged

from the hall just in time to take a swat at her younger brother as he passed. "Papa, can't you do something with him?"

"I can't see why Will would want to marry you, anyway," Rob shot back when safely out of range. "You're such a . . . a girl!" With that pronouncement, the eleven-year-old disappeared into the great outdoors to join his younger brother and sister on the lawn.

Will stared after him. He thrust his hands into his pockets, wondering the same thing.

"Well, Sally, what do you have to say about all of this?" Mr. Blythe asked his daughter. "Young Starret here has offered for you."

"I would like to be engaged to Will very much, Papa," Sally said with complete honesty. Nonetheless, she felt a twinge at being so dishonest with her parents. Two small patches of color appeared in her cheeks and she looked down at her toes with rare modesty. "I am sure that Will and I have always dealt exceedingly well together! He's my best friend!" To illustrate her point, she crossed the room and placed her hand into the crook of Will's arm. He looked down at her dubiously, and she squeezed very hard.

"Oh, yes! Best friends! Very fond of Sally! Always have been!" Awkwardly, he patted her hand.

Nonetheless, Mr. Blythe still looked a little dubious, as if something were amiss, but he would be hard pressed to put his finger on precisely what it was.

"I think it's perfectly lovely!" Mrs. Blythe said. "You know that Sir Walton and Lady Starret and your papa and I have long hoped for this match! I am sure that nothing could please us more!" As he spoke, she rang the bell, and in a moment, Ruttle, the family butler appeared.

"Ruttle, you have been with the family forever, so I need not scruple to tell you that Miss Sally and Master Will are engaged!" Mrs. Blythe said. "We will like some Madeira to celebrate, please."

It was almost as hard to accept Ruttle's congratulations as those of her mother. Even though Ruttle's manners were a great deal more formal than those of her parents, he allowed himself to defrost enough to wish them well, to recall a number of incidents from her and Will's shared childhood and to say that Cook had just baked some of the gooseberry tarts Master Will was so fond of. With this last pronouncement, he removed himself with a stately tread to inform belowstairs that Miss and her young man had finally made a go of it.

"I have informed Will of what he must already know, that Sally has received a good inheritance—"

"We can discuss the settlements later," Will said quickly. "After we come back from London!" He had the grace to look distinctly uncomfortable.

"Oh, of course you will want to go to the Metropolis for your bride clothes," Mrs. Blythe said to Sally. "Oh, dear me, where did I put the names of all those warehouses we used when Julia became engaged! Oh, and we shall have to write to all the relations, too! And I shall have to speak to the Rector about the church . . ."

"We don't intend to announce it right away!" Sally said quickly.

"No! Thought we would wait!" Will added, with a grateful look at Sally. "That is, no need to puff it off right away!" He scrambled desperately. "Father's not well!" he finally blurted out.

Mrs. Blythe looked at him from beneath the ruffle of her cap, concern reflected in her face. "Oh, dear! We just saw him Sunday last and, aside from his gout, he seemed perfectly well!"

"Does Walt have any objection to this match? I cannot believe that he would, for it has long been an object between us," Mr. Blythe said suspiciously.

"No! That is, daresay he'll be overjoyed! Haven't told him the great news yet! Health won't stand it," Will said wildly, looking at Sally for assistance.

"What Will means is that Sir Walton . . . Sir Walton's gout is very bad just now, and he cannot stand the strain of too much celebrating!" Sally said quickly.

Her father looked at her over his spectacles and cleared his throat, but merely said, "Oh?"

Mrs. Blythe, more trusting, shook her skirts. "Poor, dear Walt! Your mama told me that the least disturbance is likely to set him off! It is a great deal too bad! Of course, we will spare him the necessity of visits and parties while he is feeling so ill!" She beamed upon Will.

At that moment, Ruttle returned bearing a tray and all the best wishes of the Blythes' staff.

Will hoped his sigh of relief was not too audible.

He only wished that Mr. Blythe would not look at them as if he knew something was amiss, but could not put his finger on it!

It made him feel like a small boy who has done something wrong and is only waiting punishment for his misdeeds.

"Nonsense," Sally said when Will confided his feelings to her. "Papa *always* looks like that. You simply never noticed before. Besides, we are not precisely *lying* to our parents, you know. We *do* want to become engaged, just not married!"

But she was not without a conscience, and a visit to neighboring Crosslands, the Starret estate, resulted in large twinges of guilt.

Sir Walton, a man easily moved to emotions, wept and embraced her, careful not to dislodge his heavily bandaged foot from its gout stool, saying that this was what he had wished for all along, and that he had always loved her as much as his own dear daughters. Since this was perfectly true, it did little to assuage Sally's feelings of guilt.

He also embraced Will, thumping him heartily on the back and complimenting him on his singular good sense in adhering to the advice of his elders in his selection of a bride, calling him "a true Starret."

"Now you begin to show some sense, my boy!" Sir Walton exclaimed. "Marrying your dear mother was the making of me as a lad! Twenty-five of the happiest years of my life in wedded bliss!"

Will was so startled by this unexpected demonstration of affection from his choleric parent that he accidentally bumped into his father's gouty foot.

In the ensuing confusion, Sally and Will tried to

make their escape, but not before they were accosted by Lady Starret, who embraced Sally and her son and then presented her future daughter-in-law with the Starret family engagement ring, an old-fashioned design consisting of a large emerald surrounded by pearls and diamonds.

"All the Starret women have worn this, Sally," she said. "Walton was particularly anxious for you to have it before you left for London. My dear child, I am so pleased! I must consult with your mama at once about the ceremony! And my daughter Louisa will want to know, too! Did you know she is increasing? We just had a letter from Staverly Hall this morning! Lord Staverly is such a nervous man, so worried that he will barely allow her to stir from the house! Doubtless if she were here she could read me out for giving you such an ungainly old-fashioned piece, rather than something simpler, but I am sure that Will will want to buy you a very nice piece from Rundel & Bridge or Hamlet's when you go to town—dear me, I remember when Will and you were babies. Walton, do you recollect where we put that kit-kat of the children taken when they were babies? The one where Will is lying on the bearskin rug?"

Will sensed that his mother was going to dig up a great many embarrassing pieces of family history and unfortunately said so. This caused his father to castigate him as a lobberjack without any family feeling whatsoever, a remark punctuated with many flying gestures of his ebony cane, which he used to fine effect when his pain was at its most severe.

In order to restore the peace, Sally, much against her own inclinations, placed the ring on her finger and declared it the most beautiful piece of jewelry she had ever seen in her life, a remark that made Lady Starret stare at her in a most peculiar way.

Previously, Lady Starret had always believed that her dear friend Maria Blythe had passed her own impeccable taste on to her daughters, but that remark made her wonder.

Sally was so full of blushes, as much for her own mendacity as for the ring, that she was rendered almost speechless for the rest of the evening. It was coming over her that this may not have been such a good idea after all.

"She's overcome with emotion," Will explained.

Lady Starret patted her hand understandingly. "I have a very nice set of pearls and diamonds that you might well prefer, my dear," she suggested quietly. "They are much more in the current style."

"Oh, no!" Sally protested. "That is, family tradition is so important!" At that point she would have preferred death to accepting another gift from people who had been her second family all of her life and had never shown her anything but kindness.

"I was ready to sink into the floor when your papa offered a toast to *the best girl in the world*," she said to Will when he drove her home that night. "Oh, Will! I feel like the veriest wretch!"

"Too late to turn back now," he said glumly. "Let's just hope Quartermaine comes up to scratch."

3

As soon as Sally and Will were on the Oxford Road, headed for London, their spirits improved considerably.

Early in the morning, Will, laden with messages from his parents, had driven his phaeton over to the Blythes' house to fetch up Sally.

When he saw the pile of trunks and bandboxes Sally considered necessary to a sojourn in the Metropolis, Will's reaction was far from that of a man besotted with love.

"I say, Sal, where the deuce am I supposed to put all of this? This is a phaeton, not a traveling coach!" Will expostulated to his fiancée as he jumped down and handed his reins to a waiting footman, striding up on the shallow steps of the portico to frown down at Sally.

Sally, in a bottle-green kerseymere travel dress,

her little bronze driving hat secured with a length of gauze scarf-net, placed her hands on her hips and glared at Will impatiently. "Do you expect me to go to London with no clothes? Perhaps you think I should wear what's on my back for the next month? Really, Will, it's not that much! Just a few trunks and a bandbox or two."

Mr. Blythe emerged from his study just in time to listen to the interesting dialogue that ensued between Will and Sally. Although his expression was amused, the faint, skeptical twinkle in his eyes deepened. Meanwhile, his lady wife, several of the younger children and their governess, Mrs. Blythe's abigail, two more footmen, and the redoubtable Ruttle appeared from the nether regions of Blythe House to bid the couple safe journey.

While Sally and Will were still debating the number and amount of her bags, Ruttle and one of the footmen quietly stowed the various pieces in the boot of the phaeton, working them about in such a way as to allow them all to fit around Will's considerable belongings already installed in the vehicle.

"I don't know why you think you have to drag everything you own along to town when you know perfectly well that the first thing you and Julia will do is go shopping!" Will complained.

"That just shows what you know about it!" Sally retorted.

A prolonged farewell was enacted, during which Sally several times wondered if she had forgotten certain things and had to be restrained from searching through her luggage. Mrs. Blythe worried about highwaymen, accidents, and bad food at the inns along the journey, and had to be reassured by both Will and her spouse that the Oxford Road in bright daylight and fine weather was a safe and well-traveled thoroughfare. Will was an excellent driver, and a luncheon from the Blue Boar in Reading was hardly likely to occasion summer complaint from tainted food.

Each of Sally's younger brothers and sisters had to be hugged and promised a treat from the London toy shops upon her return. By that time, most of the staff had lined up to wish Miss Sally safe journey. Being a well brought up young lady who had known most of the servants at Blythe House since childhood, she shook each of their hands, which meant that Will, as her affianced, must also do the same, and receive their congratulations upon their engagement.

It was well past eight o'clock when they finally rolled down the drive and away toward the Oxford Road, and Will could be heard exclaiming in no uncertain terms that no, he would never allow anyone as dashed ham-hand as Sally to take the reins of his team until they reached a safe and open stretch in the road.

Miss Pruitt, the governess and a confirmed romantic, waved her handkerchief until they were out of sight and then used it to dab her eyes. "Such a handsome pair, and so well suited! Imagine, falling in love with the lad next door!"

"Oh, it is just what his mother and I have always hoped for," Mrs. Blythe said, misting a little herself. "Imagine, they have *finally* fallen in love!"

"If that's love, I'll eat my hat," Mr. Blythe said.

"Those two are no more in love than black is white!"

Mrs. Blythe turned amazed eyes on her spouse. "Why, James, why ever do you think that?" she asked. "What other reason could there be for them to announce their engagement?"

Mr. Blythe removed his spectacles and polished them along the line of his lapel. "I wish I knew," he said.

Oblivious to the hint of suspicion they had left in the bosom of Sally's parent, they pushed on toward the Metropolis. With only a stop at Reading, they were able to congratulate themselves upon making fine time, with only one or two minor spats along the way, both of them concerning Will's opinion of Sally's driving skills, or her opinion of his.

"Well, since it was you who taught me how to drive, you shouldn't be so critical," Sally said spiritedly after Will had roundly castigated her for passing the Western Mail with only inches to spare.

"I didn't teach you a move like that, by God!" Will cried. "And don't bother to repeat what the coachman said to you, either! Ladies don't use words like that!"

"But it was Alex who taught me to drive to an inch!" Sally retorted. "He is a complete hand and a nonpareil, unlike some people I know!"

"I just hope he didn't teach you to swear like Letty Lade!" Will retorted, hanging on to his hat. "Ham-handed!"

"Chicken-hearted!" Sally jeered

"By God, if I really had to marry you, I'd kill myself!" Will shouted.

"Take care you don't kill us both with *your* driving!" Sally handed him back the reins.

Since these squalls were usually full of sound and fury and passed as soon as they had arrived, by the time the phaeton drew up before the residence of Lord and Lady Tilghman on Upper Mount Street, they were both in humor again.

"Mind you don't tell Julia it's all a hum, or everyone will know! She cannot keep a secret for her life!" Sally warned Will.

"You don't need to tell me that," he replied. "Mind you don't spill it yourself!"

The Tilghman residence was no simple town house, but a very grand mansion indeed, as befitted the town residence of the scion of one of the oldest families in England. For generations, the Tilghmans had been Noted Public Men, devoting their lives and their careers to the interests of the country. During the reign of the late Lord Tilghman especially, it had seen many grand entertainments and many Important Persons, including royalties from several countries.

Aurora, Dowager Countess Tilghman, however, had seen fit to claim many of the house's furnishings as her own upon her reluctant departure to only somewhat less elegant surroundings in Grosvenor Square. Her son George, the present Lord Tilghman, adapting the philosophy "anything to keep the peace," had allowed her to carry away several cartloads of furniture, plate, tapestry, rugs, and porcelain, promising his new bride that she could do exactly as she wished in refurbishing Tilghman House.

Julia, the present Lady Tilghman, terrified, like most folk, of her formidable mother-in-law, was secretly relieved to be rid of so much dowdy old stuff, some of which dated back to the reign of Queen Anne. With unlimited funds at her disposal and an indulgent and very busy husband, she had set about redoing the old pile with a will.

A somewhat naive young debutante, Julia had found that the position of married lady suited her very well. Acknowledged as a Beauty, secure in her place as the countess of an earl with a very handsome fortune, it was not long before she was seeking the advice of some of the most fashionable people in London on her decorating schemes, as well as employing some of the city's most distinguished craftsmen. Frequently, the opinions of these two groups of people clashed, and the result was that, even after twelve months, a great portion of Tilghman House remained disrupted by carpenters, paperhangers, mercers, upholsterers, and other more esoteric artisans, none of whom seemed in any great hurry to complete their allotted tasks.

Of a consequence, life with the Tilghmans could sometimes be a catch as catch can affair. On her last visit, Mrs. Blythe had found herself taking tea with a man who turned out to be a silk merchant's assistant, there to take measurements for the Green Drawing Room's curtains. "But he seemed like such a gentleman!" she exclaimed later. "*Perfectly* genteel. Besides, he told me where I could get satins at only twelve shillings the yard! I thought he was just one of Julia's counter-coxcomb friends, for men like that can always be depended to know such things!"

Unfortunately, Julia had not inherited her mother's taste or her father's understanding. Also, it must be noted that her friends, while fashionable, were not always wise. Those rooms that had been completed were sometimes known to startle the unwary visitor.

"Wonder what she's done to the place now," Will wondered aloud to Sally as he handed her down from the phaeton. Wisely, he left the unloading of Sally's possessions to the pair of elegant footmen who emerged from the house.

Today, a new butler, quite different from the last two, answered the door. Introducing himself as Tweed, he led Miss Blythe and Mr. Starret through scenes of construction and holland covers before ushering them into a startling midnight-blue room full of gilt furniture, carved with the heads and feet of lions and crocodiles, all of the room smelling very strongly of plaster and fresh paint. Bidding them wait while he went away to summon her ladyship, Tweed stumbled away.

"I think he's drunk!" Sally murmured to Will, who was leaning up against the mantel, until he realized his elbow was resting in the open mouth of a carved lion, and he jerked it away.

"I wouldn't doubt it," he replied with some sympathy, rubbing his coat sleeve. "You'd want to be foxed, living in this mess!" At that moment, a familiar voice floated down the hall.

"No! No, absolutely not! All of that dreadful green will have to be ripped out! It makes me look bilious, and I will *not* look bilious in my own breakfast room! Now, the white-and-yellow striped wallpaper, I think—Sally! Will!"

Julia did not merely enter a room; she made an entrance. Surrounded by a furry of wallpaper merchants and drapers, she sailed across the blue and gilt room toward them, both hands extended. One still clutched a scrap of Nile green brocade and a strip of figured Tyrian purple wallpaper. This did not stop her from embracing first her sister, then her friend.

She was very much in looks, but then there was never a time when Julia was not in looks. Beneath an ornate and lacy morning cap, curls of warm honey-colored hairlay in a charming manner about her creamy cheeks, tinged with just a hint of a rose blush. Eyes as large and blue as sapphires were framed by long brown lashes. A perfect little mouth turned up in a smile. Her graceful figure was shown to advantage by a pretty morning dress with a great many pleats and ruffles in an ivory muslin, trimmed with pale blue ribbons. Her tiny feet were encased in blue silk slippers.

"Oh, my dears, I am so glad to see you! There is so much gossip about, you would not believe! Wait until I tell you all the latest on-dits! How was your journey? How are Mama and Papa and all the brats? Would you believe I actually miss the children? And how is Louisa? I had a letter from her, so I know she has good news! Imagine being buried in Hampshire for your entire confinement!

But she likes the country! How are Sir Walton and Lady Starret? Are you taking your old rooms in Pall Mall, Will? What's this?"

As she spoke, she picked up Sally's hand, where the large, old-fashioned ring now took up a great deal of her fourth finger. "I see we are buying emeralds now! Whatever next?"

When she paused to take a breath, Sally said, "It's the Starret family engagement ring!"

"My lady, we really must have a decision on the upholstery color now!" one of the tradesmen said.

"Lady Tilghman, do you want the Lightfoot carved paneling in the dining room or in the reception room?"

"My lady—"

"Ma'am, I must insist—"

All of them, including Will, fell back as Julia uttered a piercing shriek. "You're engaged! Oh, I don't believe it!"

"Well, it's true!" Will said defensively. "Why wouldn't it be true? Perfectly natural thing to do, after all."

"Will—" Sally hissed, but she was gathered into a celebratory embrace before she could say anything more.

"I'm so excited for you! You were *made* for each other!" Julia cried. "Oh, this is so exciting! Everyone knew you two would finally fall in love!"

"Oh, yes!" Sally said quickly, acutely aware of the stares of the interested tradesmen.

Julia admired her ring. She did not find it excessive or old fashioned and sighed that Tilghman had given her a set of pearls as an engagement present.

"The Dowager is still clutching all the good family pieces," she added, much to the interest of those witnessing this performance.

"Julia, don't you want to finish your business with all of these people?" Sally asked a little desperately.

"Oh!" Julia, calmed herself, reasserted her dignity, thrusting the wallpaper and the brocade into the hands of the nearest person. "All of you go on and do whatever you were doing, if you please! I will be with you directly!" She made shooing motions with her hands, as if they were a flock of unruly chickens, and the tradesman retreated, bowing themselves out the door.

"For what Tilghman is paying them, they can afford to wait for a while," she confided airily. "I don't think this house will *ever* be done, but then if it's in an uproar, I don't have to entertain Important People. You are so lucky not to know any Important People, they're so very dull! Tilghman seems to know nothing *but* statesmen and politicians and the most prosy sort of people! Fortunately, I have been making some much more interesting friends, people who are ever so much more amusing, who couldn't care less about M. Talleyrand or the Tsar or politics!" A slight edge had crept into her voice, and Sally swiftly changed the subject.

"This is the most amazing room! Why, I feel as if I am inside an astrolabe!"

"Bein' attacked by crocodiles," Will muttered. "Ouch!"

Sally had kicked him in the shin. "Oh, Will likes it, too!" she said brightly.

Will looked at his fiancée in a way that was far from loverlike. "It's very . . . interesting," he said at last.

Julia beamed at them both. "I believe I have quite a talent for decorating, don't you think? Wait until you see your bedchamber, Sally, it's lavender and yellow with splashes of green!"

"I can't wait!" Sally murmured.

"Tell me how all this comes about! The last time I talked to you, you both swore that you both would never get married!" Julia cried. "At least to each other. I thought it was very ill-considered of our parents to keep throwing you together in hopes you would make a match of it! There could be nothing calculated to drive you further apart!" She gestured them to sit on a blue and gold striped sofa whose arms and legs were the paws and jaws of caimans and plumped herself down opposite them, all ears.

"That's true enough," Will gingerly settled himself with an uneasy glance at the gilt reptile mouth uncomfortably close to his arm. "Always sayin' to me, 'why don't you take Sally for a drive?' Or 'Why don't you ask Sally to waltz?' Like dancin' with Louisa!"

"And you know how Mama goes on, 'Sally, be sure and leave a space on your dance card for Will,' or 'Sally, idle hands are the devil's plaything. Why don't you knit a muffler or a pair of sturdy stockings for Will?' till I was ready to scream," Sally confided. "Well, of course, I love Will, he's been like a brother to me, but—"

"As if I would wear a pair of stockings *you* knitted. Ham-handed, that's what you are! By God,

Jules, you should have seen her take the reins today! Almost scraped the paint off the Great Western Mail! Any female who drives like that can't possibly knit!"

"Ham-handed, am I?" Sally cried indignantly, picking up a cushion embroidered with acanthus leaves and tossing it at Will. "Well, I wish you could have seen yourself, my man, rolling out of the Blue Boar on a hitched lead!"

"I never did!" Will shook his head. He tossed the pillow back at Sally, who caught it neatly.

Julia looked from one to the other. A faint spark of disbelief shone in her eyes. "Getting engaged doesn't seem to have changed you two in the least," she said brightly. "You're still squabbling like cats and dogs!"

"Us?" Will asked. "Come on, Jules!"

"We're *deeply* in love!" Sally protested, moving a few inches closer to Will on the sofa.

Will looked at her, then put his arm uneasily around her shoulders. "Madly, truly deeply in love!" he added.

"Isn't love grand?" A lazy voice drawled from the doorway.

Alex Quartermaine entered the room. He was tall and dark and handsome in the Byronic fashion so very much in style. Raven curls, cut in the Brutus style were carefully styled around his nobly-shaped forehead; heavy lids shaded his piercing blue eyes, which regarded the company with amusement. A patrician Roman nose, full, sensual lips, right now curving in a crooked smile completed a handsome countenance, supported by a high collar and a snowy cravat tied in the *trône d'amour.* His well-tailored corbeau coat of Bath superfine needed no padding to compliment his broad shoulders and slender waist; his biscuit-hued breeches were molded to muscular thighs and well-shaped calves. Several fobs and seals depended from the watch chain on his embroidered waistcoat, and his top boots gleamed in the dim afternoon light.

Sally felt her heart leap in her breast. What woman could have resisted such a virile example of male pulchritude? Certainly not the Blythe sisters, whose twin expressions took on a fleeting wishful cast. A set of twin sighs were felt, but not heard. The Blythe sisters were well brought up young ladies, but they were not immune to masculine elegance.

And what Corinthian could not help but feel a faint revulsion at the scent of Alex's musky cologne? Will bit his lower lip and frowned. Alex's charm was lost on the male sex.

Having allowed himself a second in the doorway for the ladies to admire him, Alex sauntered into the room. "One of the workmen let me in. I fear your butler is nowhere to be found, Julia."

"Alex! You are just in time to hear the news," Julia exclaimed, jumping up to greet him. "Sally and Will are engaged! You do know Mr. Starret, don't you?"

"Ah?" he said, still smiling.

Alex bowed toward Will and approached Sally, taking both of her hands into his own. As he bent toward her, his blue eyes seemed to bore into hers, and his faint, crooked smile grew even more quizzical. Lightly, he kissed the air above her hands, and she felt herself flush up to the roots of her hair.

Holding her fingers just a moment longer than necessary, he said, "Allow me to congratulate you! I must confess myself a bit startled by your news, since when I came in, you were tossing a pillow at Will!" He shook his head. "Not at all a loverlike gesture, wouldn't you think? My, what a quaint ring! A family piece, perhaps?"

"Couldn't care less what you think, old man," Will said, crossing his arms firmly across his chest.

"Don't be rude, Will!" Sally said. She disengaged her fingers from Alex's grasp and made a small show of moving closer to Will and tucking her hand into the crook of his arm. Will raised one eyebrow and opened his mouth, then closed it swiftly. He patted Sally's hand and glared fiercely at Alex.

"Sorry," Will muttered in a surly voice. "Very much in love with Sally! Daresay we shall deal very well together!"

"Oh, I have no doubt of that," Alex replied lightly in the same mocking tone. He lifted his quizzing glass to one eye and glanced at Will's driving boots for a brief moment before turning his attention to Julia.

"My dear, forgive me for dropping by unannounced in such a family moment! This must come to both of us as a surprise!"

He sat down in a crocodile chair and crossed one elegant leg over the other, smiling beatifically at Sally and Will. "The happy couple! What domestic bliss there will be!" he said.

"I am sure we shall suit!" Sally replied in a tight voice. "Will is the most romantic man! He treats me like a princess!"

"Not, one hopes, like poor Princess Charlotte," Alex drawled. "The latest on-dit is that the Regent has made her a virtual prisoner at Chartwood, all because she went to see her mother!"

"No!" Julia exclaimed, diverted. "What does Princess Caroline say?"

"Well, I saw Miss Mercer Elphinstone at the Millbanks last night, and she was full of news," Alex said.

Now that his complete attention was on Julia, Sally relaxed her grip on Will's sleeve slightly.

He pulled out his watch. "Uh, really ought to get going. Don't like to leave my horses standing like this, don't you know," he said as he rose from the sofa. "My people will be wondering what happened to me if I don't check in soon at my digs."

"Oh, must you leave so soon?" Sally asked, throwing Will a speaking look.

Will frowned. He was at a loss to determine what she wanted until she turned her cheek toward him. Dutifully, he leaned over and kissed her.

"I'll see you in a day or so," he promised vaguely, making his farewells to Julia and Mr. Quartermaine.

Will exited, feeling a great sense of relief.

On the steps, however, he encountered Lord Tilghman, who, on his way into his own home, had stopped to admire the matched bays that pulled Will's phaeton.

George, the eleventh Lord Tilghman was a few

years his wife's senior, which made him seem rather old to Will. The false impression of middle age was enhanced by his rather formal manners and the premature streaks of silver at his temples, as well as the aristocratic, aquiline features that were the distinguishing characteristic of the Tilghman family. Those who knew him well appreciated his dry wit and his generosity of spirit and purse.

After exchanging greetings, Tilghman and Will immediately fell into an involved discussion of the various points of Will's team, then horses in general. After the equine topic was thoroughly covered, the conversation ranged over the forthcoming hunting and gunning seasons, and from there, an exhaustive discussion of the various sporting entertainments offered at this Season in town followed, Lord Tilghman promising Mr. Starret that he would put in a good word for him at Jackson's Boxing Saloon, perhaps even create a chance for a round or two with Gentleman Jackson himself. It was only after the comparative merits of the Albany and Pall Mall as the ideal lodgings for a bachelor had been debated that Will remembered to tell Tilghman that he had gotten engaged to Sally.

The reaction was not what he had expected at all.

"Sally's a fine girl, but I wouldn't be in a great hurry to get buckled if I was you," Tilghman said with a shuddering look at his own house. "Treasure your bachelor days while you have them, my boy!"

Taken by surprise, Sally sat mesmerized, watching and listening to Alex Quartermaine. He was, she thought, even more handsome than she remembered, and her memories were filtered through a rosy haze. Simply being in his presence again was like finding water after a long trek across the desert.

All of her careful resolutions, that she would not wear her heart upon her sleeve, that she would be cool and distantly civil, seemed to be melting in the face of the reality. Her heart was thundering so loudly that she was sure Alex would hear it across the room, and she wished she could change into another dress and comb her hair.

She had every reason to excuse herself from the room and wait for a more opportune time to present itself, yet her feet seemed to be rooted to the floor, and her tongue so tied that all she could do was giggle witlessly at his conversation.

Fool! she castigated herself.

But Alex barely seemed to notice. He had embarked upon a long, involved story about a group of people Sally did not know. It was quite clear that Julia did know them, for her eyes sparkled and from time to time, she gave a small, titillated shriek and pressed her hand to her bosom.

"I say, Quartermaine, do you live here?" Tilghman asked without preamble as he entered his wife's drawing room.

It was as if a cloud had descended upon the heads of Julia and Alex. Although they had been leaning together very closely, they drew back and their smiles disappeared.

"You would think Tilghman could greet his sister-in-law, couldn't you?" Julia asked irritably as she smoothed down her skirts.

"Indeed I can," Tilghman replied, bending to kiss Sally's cheek and receive her embrace in turn. "You are looking very fine, my dear. And I understand I am to offer you my felicitations," he added.

Sally, who was sincerely fond of her brother-in-law, smiled up at him. "However did you know?" she asked.

"Saw young Will on his way out," Tilghman replied, seating himself beside her. "Fine fellow, Will Starret. Daresay you will be very happy with him."

"It is so rare that one sees a couple so ideally matched," Alex said with his sardonic smile. He rose to his feet, regarding himself discreetly in the mirror over the mantel. Apparently satisfied with what he saw, he flicked an invisible piece of lint from his lapel and bowed toward Julia. "I shall call for you at nine," he promised.

"I rather thought you would be staying in tonight, since it is your sister's first night in town," Tilghman said gently.

Julia frowned, a tiny downward curve of her brows, a little thrust of her lower lip. "But I accepted Mrs. Paige's invitation weeks ago, before I knew when Sally would be here. All fashionable London will be there! I can't cry off now. Sally understands, don't you, dear? It's a loo party!"

"Of course," Sally said politely. Nothing could have bored her more than an evening of card playing, nor the sort of people she could easily predict would be there.

"I, of course, will be escorting Julia, but I hope that I shall have the opportunity to see you again, soon, Sally," Alex said.

"Oh, I am sure we shall meet from time to time," Sally replied, pleased with the vagueness of her reply. And, she had to admit, just a little jealous that Alex seemed to have ingratiated himself with her sister.

"Good day, Quartermaine," Tilghman said pleasantly.

Alex, with no other choice, made his farewells.

He was no sooner out of the room than Julia, too rose. "I should show you up to your room, Sally," she said quickly. "I imagine you would like to rest after your journey, wouldn't you."

"Perhaps you would like to accompany me to the

theater, tonight, Sally," Tilghman said, not unkindly. "It's that Keane fella all the females are swooning over. I'd purchased two tickets thinking my wife might join me."

"Edmund Keane! Oh, Tilghman," Sally cried. "You are the best of brothers-in-law!"

It was only after she was in her room, watching the maid unpack her clothes that Sally realized that her sister and her brother-in-law had not spoken a word to each other.

Perhaps, she thought, divesting herself of her travel-dusted pelisse, she had been mistaken. No one, she reflected, could have been more in love with each other than Tilghman and Julia. It had been universally declared a love match when they had wedded the previous year amid much celebration and many guests. Although she had barely been out of the schoolroom during their courtship, even she had been able to tell that this was not one of her beautiful sister's flirts when Tilghman had first come to visit Blythe House.

During her interrupted Season, when she and Mama had stayed with Julia and Tilghman, her older sister had dropped a great many lofty hints that the married state was one of intimate bliss. So much so that Mama had finally clapped her hands over Sally's ears and declared Julia a great wretch for exposing an innocent child to such details of marital intimacy. Sally, who had at that point, only received the most basic instruction in the facts of life, was enthralled with Julia's revelations, although she found it difficult to think of Tilghman in terms of a passionate lover. At thirty, he seemed much too old to be romantic, at least to Sally. Still, it was a simple matter for her to use her newfound, if secondhand, knowledge to imagine herself and Alex Quartermaine in a similar situation. Mrs. Blythe would have been horrified to know how much of the past year her second daughter had spent daydreaming about Alex's arms about her, Alex's lips on hers . . .

Sally looked out the window at Upper Mount Street. In spite of the late coming of darkness in these last days of summer, the lamplighter was already making his early rounds with his ladder and staff, and couples, already dressed for evening, were emerging from their houses and disappearing into elegant carriages, ready to begin the night's round of festivities. From St. Margaret's, the church bells tolled vespers. She felt as if the city lay spread out below her like a jewel, ready for her to seize it, and a great sense of hope and new beginnings came over her.

She would marry Alex, she would! She knew she would! This little deception, which weighed as heavily on her conscience as the Starret ring on her finger, would prove worthwhile. Now that she had seen Alex again, if only for a moment, she just *knew* she could win him. The how and when had yet to come to her, but with the optimism of youth, she knew she could win his heart back to her!

Thinking of Alex made her sigh, and she quivered a little with anticipation and lay down to have her nap with a blissful smile on her lips.

When she awakened, it was dark enough that

long blue shadows were stealing through the chinks in the curtains, and the street outside was quiet; only the jingle and clop of a solitary carriage echoed up to her bedchamber. Thinking to have a sisterly chat with Julia, she dragged a comb through her hair and walked down the hallway. The upper stories at least had been completed in a modern manner, and Sally was sure that the tole-print wallpaper, featuring a great deal of *chinoiserie*, was very fashionable, but it made her a little dizzy. So many fat little men in so many little pagodas over looking so many little lakes, so many willowy ladies in kimonos standing on so many bridges looking into so many streams! She was not terribly certain about the enormous Delft flower pagodas, overlooked by the Dowager, that were set into recesses in the hall every few yards, either, but assumed that this, too, must be very fashionable.

She found Julia in her dressing room, holding her breath while her abigail laced her into her stays. "I can't understand it," Julia was saying. "I eat like a bird, and I still seem to be getting a thick waist. Try it again, Pomfret."

Miss Pomfret, a plump, bustling sort of female, wrapped the measure around her mistress's waist. "Twenty inches," she said. "Still twenty inches. You don't suppose, my lady that you're—" when she saw Sally standing in the doorway, she broke off, curtseying. "Oh, Miss! You gave me such a turn! I didn't hear you knock!"

"Hello, Pomfret," Sally greeted her cheerfully. "It's nice to see you again!"

Pomfret smiled, for she was fond of her mistress's younger sister, whose presence enlivened the house considerably. "And it's very nice to see you, too, I'm sure! I've saved you all the latest issues of *La Belle Assemblé* and *The Ladies' Magazine.* The new autumn styles should be very becoming to you." She gestured toward a pile of journals lying on a chest, and with a happy cry, Sally fell on them.

She ensconced herself on the chaise and immediately began browsing through the pages, scanning the fashion prints as she and her sister talked.

"I think we need to have M. Durran come in and cut Miss Sally's hair, don't you?" Julia asked. "Styles are for more curls this Season, and she needs a new touch."

"Maybe he can tone down my poor fiery head," Sally giggled, twirling a lock of her copper hair around a finger and studying it dubiously.

"Good God, no!" Julia said, much shocked. "Mama would have a fit if you dyed your hair! Only *very* fast women do that!"

From the clothespress, Pomfret withdrew a shimmering evening dress of pomona green silk, overlaid with a spider-web gauze half skirt trimmed in ivory crepe. She dropped it over Julia's head and began the slow process of working it down over her corselet, making sure that the delicate pleats and runchings were not wrinkled.

"I really am sorry about this, Sally, but you see how it is," Julia's voice, muffled, rose from the froth of silk and gauze. "I have to go, Sally, I really must. You see how it is."

Suddenly, her head emerged from the dress, and Sally looked up to meet her sister's eyes. Did she detect some hint of desperation in that beautiful face?

Again, she recalled that Tilghman and Julia had not spoken a word to each other earlier, and a vague suspicion that all was not well crossed her mind. If Pomfret had not been there, Sally would have launched into an intense sisterly inquisition. As things were, she waited to see what hints and cues Julia threw out.

But Julia was evidently not in the mood for revelations of any sort, for she threw a rather strained smile at Sally and tilted her head, as if challenging her to believe the fashionable Lady Tilghman's life was less than perfect.

Sally looked down at the journal in her lap, unwilling to pursue the matter. It suddenly occurred to her that Julia, for her part, might ask some very awkward questions about her engagement to Will.

The conversation turned toward the latest fashions, and Sally watched as her sister and Pomfret went through the elaborate ritual of turning my lady out for an evening card party.

When Pomfret at last pronounced Lady Tilghman ready to appear in Society and draped a filmy shawl over her shoulders, Julia smiled the small brittle smile and kissed Sally on the cheek. "You do understand, my dear, I *have* to go to this party." Pomfret adjusted one of her diamond ear drops, clucking her tongue. "I'm obligated, you see," Julia sighed.

"Of course," Sally replied. "Please don't worry

about it. Just let me know what Alex says about my engagement."

"Oh, that's right," Julia said vaguely, turning a bracelet on her arm. "You were one of his flirts before you left town, weren't you?"

Sally felt as if she had been stung. "One of his flirts," she repeated dully.

The sound of the bell pealed through the house.

"Oh, that's Alex now. Listen, darling, I really must go now, but tomorrow, we'll go shopping and have a nice long comfortable cose, all right?"

She was gone in a rustle of silk and a faint scent of lily-of-the-valley lingering on the air.

Sally looked at the abigail, but Miss Pomfret, her features deliberately expressionless, bustled about, straightening up. Sally might not be above gossiping with the servants, especially one as loyal as Pomfret, but the abigail was determinedly loyal to her mistress.

"I asked my lady to have Betty assist you while you're here, Miss," she said. "She's a smart girl and clever with her sewing. Let me know if she doesn't suit. My lady employed her as a chambermaid, but she's anxious to improve her station in the world."

"Oh, yes, I am sure we will deal very well together," Sally agreed, but she lingered a moment amid the crumpled tissue and spilled powder.

"Time's getting on, Miss. My lord doesn't like to be late to the theater," Miss Pomfret said.

And with that strong hint in her ears, Sally took herself off to her own room.

● ● ●

When Sally came into the drawing room an hour later, it was to find Tilghman slumped by the fireplace, a glass of wine in his hand. He was staring moodily into the flame, but when he saw Sally enter the room, he stood up and smiled.

"Well, my girl," he said. "You are looking very fetching tonight, I must say."

Sally smiled, knowing that she would never be a fashion plate like her sister. But she thought herself turned out very credibly in a theater dress of straw-colored silk, trimmed in contrasting bands of canary silk cording. Her hair was dressed à la Aphrodite, and she wore her pearl set.

After a supper at the Piazza, they proceeded to the theater. Tilghman had procured a box, and for upward of a half hour, Sally sat enthralled by her favorite actor, Edmund Keane, while Tilghman enjoyed her pleasure more than the noted actor's histrionics. Perhaps he was thinking of a time when Julia and he enjoyed such simple entertainments.

When he was least expecting it, Sally plucked on his sleeve and asked in a whisper if the young female playing the ingenue was Miss Quinn?

Upon Lord Tilghman's assenting that the vivacious brunette was indeed Miss Quinn, Sally blurted, "Oh, she's the one who has Will all a twitter! With her fan, she pointed to the stalls. "And look, there Will is, ogling her!"

Tilghman, by no means a prude, still shot her an amazed look, then followed her gesturing fan toward a place in the stalls below, where Mr. Starret, together with his friend Barney sat, alternately flirting with the orange girls and staring at Miss Quinn's well-shaped legs encased in the breeches required by her role. She was, Sally thought critically, a very pretty young woman of about nineteen, with a winning smile and a great deal of dark hair. She seemed to be enjoying herself thoroughly on the stage, very much aware of her admirers in the stalls, of which Will and Barney seemed to be only two to judge by the calls and whistles whenever she spoke or danced.

Oblivious to Tilghman's amazed stare, Sally smiled with amusement and continued to enjoy the play.

"You are a most unusual female, Sally," Tilghman said when the curtain had come down on the second act. "If Julia had seen me at the theatre setting up a flirt, she would have torn me limb from limb from sheer jealousy."

"But Will is only following fashion," Sally replied quickly. "It would seem that admiring Miss Quinn is quite the thing to do for young men! He doesn't mean anything by it, I am sure!"

Tilghman shook his head over the morals and manners of the coming generation. It seemed like a remarkably cavalier attitude to him.

While he was thinking these thoughts, Sally noticed a lady in a box on the opposite side of the theatre smiling and nodding in their direction. She was well past her first youth and a little plump, but still attractive. Sally turned toward her brother-in-law.

"Tilghman, there is a lady over there who seems to be trying to get your attention. Who is she?"

Tilghman looked up, then smiled. "Why, that's Marietta Rockhall!" he exclaimed. "She's the widow of Lord Rockhall, the famous diplomat, and a very important hostess, a great friend of mine. Come, let me make you known to her."

Although she had been hoping to catch Will's eye, in order to signal him to come and visit her box, she dutifully followed Tilghman along the corridor toward Lady Rockhall's box.

It seemed to be as full as it could hold already, with a number of bejeweled ladies and be-medaled gentlemen congregated there, talking and laughing on terms of great familiarity in an easy mix of English and French. Sally had had enough knowledge of Tilghman's work in the Foreign Office to recognize several diplomats, as well as one or two ambassadors and their lady ambassadresses. Count and Countess Lieven and Princess Esterhazy she knew from Almack's and was gratified when the Russian ambassadress recalled her name and reminded the princess that they must send vouchers for Tilghman's little sister-in-law. When Tilghman presented Sally to Lady Rockhall, she smiled and offered her hand, saying she had heard that Lady Tilghman had a sister and inquiring after Julia in very civil manner. She was probably in her mid-forties, with dark brown hair and a delicate olive complexion. Her dark eyes were very shrewd and there was a hint of amusement in the set of her lips. She wore a very fine diamond parure and a black silk gown. There was an aura about her of power, and of a woman accustomed to command.

"So very kind of you to come and meet me," she said, and Sally had the feeling that she had been thoroughly inspected. "I believe me have a a mutual friend in Alexander Quartermaine."

Sally mustered a smile, a trifle flustered. "Oh, yes, Alex is a particular friend of mine," she said.

Those dark eyes held her for a moment, then dropped to the emerald on her finger. The finely arched black brows lifted almost imperceptibly. "Alex tells me that you are engaged," she offered.

Sally nodded. "It's not quite official yet," she murmured, wanting to know how this very grand lady knew Alex and feeling too intimidated to ask.

"A very handsome piece. One rarely sees emeralds of that water anymore. Tilghman, will you do me the honor to bring Miss Blythe and her fiancé to one of my evenings? I shall send you a card."

Her attention was claimed by Princess Esterhazy, and Tilghman, after speaking in intense French for some moments to a gentleman with a great many medals on his sash, finally bowed them both out of the box.

"Was that so difficult?" he asked, when they were on their way back to their own box.

"No," Sally said. "It was very interesting. Who is Lady—"

"Then why can't your sister take the time to do it?" Tilghman asked.

Before Sally had to think of either a question or an answer, they were back in their own box and the curtain was rising on the second act.

5

Sally awakened to the sound of hammering, and realized that the workmen started early at Tilghman House. She buried her head in her pillow but to no avail. She was awake for the day. Remembering that she was in London, and that Alex was in the same city, she felt wide awake, with the world as her oyster.

Having spent a great deal of her last days at home sending advance notice of her impending visit to her London friends, Sally had already received several cards of invitation addressed to her at Upper Mount Street. Only a small part of her motive had been to allow Alex to hear about this interesting news second hand. Nonetheless, she was gratified to find the honor of her company requested at a number of parties, dances, routs, and riddotos. At some of these, Alex would doubtless be present, she reflected happily, quite forgetting for the moment that news of her engagement to Will must be making the rounds.

Betty, her new maid, a broad-faced country girl with a ready smile, had delivered more cards on her breakfast tray, together with the news that my lady was just waking up, having come in very late, and that my lord had already left for the Foreign Office, and would Miss like her bath drawn?

Tilghman, who believed in progress, had caused the new gas lights to be installed in the house, but also piped plumbing. One of the results was a large, shell-shaped receptacle in a small room off the boudoir that could be filled with water pumped up from the kitchen regions and heated with a small gas jet.

"It didn't seem quite Christian at first somehow, Miss," Betty told her cheerfully. "But once you get used to it, it does save a lot of work, hauling those jars up and down the stairs. And you saw how it makes a world of difference in the closet under the stairs. No more emptying the chamber pots. You pull a chain and it's all gone!" Betty wrinkled her nose. "It makes an awful roar, though," she added confidentially. "If you'd rather have a chamber pot, I'd understand."

She dropped a curtsey. "Miss Pomfret says you might like to have me as your abigail, Miss. I'll do my best to give satisfaction. Miss Pomfret's been training me. I can do hair, mend and sew a dress, and iron without scorching . . . most of the time!" She swallowed. "And I'm not one who gossips

about my mistress's business belowstairs! Miss
Pomfret said that I was to tell you that a lady's
maid must be discreet!"

"Betty, I think you and I shall deal together very
well," Sally laughed.

Betty beamed and dropped another curtsey. "I'd
better light your bath, Miss; it takes a while for the
water to heat. I pressed a sprig muslin for you; it's
going to be a warm day and Miss Pomfret says my
lady will want to take you shopping!"

An hour later, turned out by Betty for a day's
expedition, Sally tripped down the hall and
knocked on her sister's door.

She found Julia dressed to go out, but seated at
her desk regarding a piece of paper with several
columns of figures, a rather harried look on her
face. At the sight of Sally, however, she smiled and
quickly shoved the piece of paper into a drawer, rising to her feet.

"Shopping is the first thing we must do today,
before you go anywhere," she told her sister a little
too brightly.

Sally said nothing as they went down the stairs
and were carried away to Oxford Street in grand
style in Lady Tilghman's barouche. Preoccupied as
she was with thoughts of when she might next see
Alex, she did not give Julia's absorption much heed.

After a year of mourning clothes, starting with
deepest black and moving into light grays and
mauves, going back into colors again was exciting
for Sally. Inveterate shoppers, both she and Julia
entered into the endeavor with enthusiasm,

descending upon Madam Celeste, London's most fashionable modiste with a determination to buy.

The end of the war had meant that the latest modes from Paris were once again available in England, and both Julia and Sally were determined to make the most of this.

Skirts were shorter and fuller, stiffened with deep, heavily ornamented hems. The waist had dropped, sleeves were growing larger, and all manner of trim was very much in fashion. Colors were back and the brighter, the better. The current passion for all things Scottish, inspired by the Waverly Novels, meant that plaids were coming into vogue, Celeste informed her clients; so very nice for autumn and winter!

But Julia's eye had already fallen on an evening dress of coral crepe with an overskirt of peach Urling's net, the corsage, sleeves, and skirt ornamented with several rouleaux of coral sarcenet and trimmed with pearls and coral beads. The price, a hefty eight hundred pounds did not seem to deter her at all, although Sally was somewhat dubious about coral complimenting Julia's coloring.

"What does it matter?" Julia said. "I think it looks wonderful! I must try it on immediately! And that bottle-green carriage dress, too, if you please! And that ivory muslin morning dress. And the blue satin, too."

It was all Celeste could do not to jump for joy. When in the proper mood, my lady was a buyer whose man of business paid her bills promptly. Nothing was too good for such a client, and even though the blue was promised to another client, Celeste graciously allowed her to try it on.

Sally might have become an heiress, but she was used to spending far more cautiously than her sister. Although she liked several of the creations Celeste presented for her inspection, she knew that she could refurbish a number of her own dresses to suit the current style far more cheaply. But even prudent Sally found herself unable to resist a pelisse of Spanish green kerseymere, trimmed with white ermine, with an enormous ermine muff to match. She could see herself riding along in Alex's phaeton on a winter's day looking very dashing indeed. Perhaps add a toque of Naples velvet with a few plumes, she thought, and her little black jean half boots.

A jaconet muslin beneath an open robe of worked blond lace she must have, too; she could see herself walking in the Park in just that dress, with its fashionable French cuffs falling over the hands. A ball dress, all blond lace over celestial blue Gofre crepe, trimmed with quilled flounces and rouleaux of satin forget-me-nots and pearls, was just what she could wear to Almack's to waltz with Alex.

An evening dress of silver foil, with an ivory openwork skirt of letting-in lace, through which bands of silver foil and ivory whitework ribbon had been worked had caught her fancy. The corsage was ivory Urling's net over silver foil, trimmed with ivory silk roses, and the gigot sleeves and deep hem were trimmed with lozenges of silver foil and bouquets of tiny ivory silk rosebuds and cockleshells.

One of Celeste's many minions had come from the workroom, carrying it over her arm, but Julia gave a small cry and halted her immediately, all but snatching up the gown and holding it against her bodice as she examined herself in the mirror, cooing in delight.

"Oh, it's lovely! Look, Sally, is this not the most fetching dress you have ever seen in your life?" she asked, turning this way and that to study herself in the pier glass.

"It is lovely," Sally agreed. "But don't you think it's just a bit much?"

"Not at all!" Julia replied. Her eyes were glazed over and she had that determined set to her mouth that meant her mind was made up.

Madam Celeste gently disengaged Julia's fingers from the shoulders of the gown. "It is a lovely dress," she agreed. "But not quite in your style, my lady! It was created with another lady in mind."

"I think it is very much in my style," Julia replied a little imperiously.

Madam Celeste cleared her throat uncomfortably. "It is spoken for, my lady. Lady Rockhall has just decided to purchase it."

"Indeed I have," said that lady as she emerged from the back of the atelier, drawing on her gloves. She smiled at Julia, who drew back as if she had been slapped. The dress slid from her fingers to the floor.

Madam Celeste and the assistant quickly rescued the gown. "I think I might have something more in your style, Lady Tilghman, if you could just step into the next room with me," the modiste said quickly.

Lady Rockhall tilted her head, a faint, amused smile playing on her lips. In the light of day, she looked older and just a little jaded. "Good morning, Lady Tilghman. Miss Blythe, I see you are shopping. I'm so sorry, but I have already purchased this dress, as you can see! I plan to wear it to a little ball I am giving. Perhaps Tilghman told you? It is for the new Swedish ambassador, you know."

"I suppose I had heard something about it," Julia said stiffly.

Lady Rockhall inclined her head. "I shall make sure that Miss Blythe receives a card of invitation together with yours! And her fiancé, who I have not yet met, but Tilghman assures me is a most worthy young man. I shall look forward to meeting him."

With that, she bowed and swept past them out of the room.

The color had drained from Julia's face, and she laughed a little. "I think we have purchased enough dresses for now!" she said unsteadily. "If you could be so good as to wrap these and send them to Tilghman House, Celeste, we will be on our way."

"What in the world was that all about?" Sally demanded as soon as she and Julia were settled back into the barouche.

Julia, still as white as a sheet, leaned her head back against the seat and closed her eyes. "That woman!" she cried, and suddenly burst into tears.

"My husband thinks I don't know, but I do! Her name is Marietta Rockhall, and she's quite old!"

"But I met her at the theater last night! She's most respectable! You must be wrong, Julia!" Sally exclaimed involuntarily.

Julia turned all the way around in her seat and grasped her sister's arms. Her face was as tight and bloodless as a mask. "He introduced you to her? My innocent sister? Oh, lord, is there no depth to which that man will not sink? How *could* he?"

"Julia Sophia Blythe, take hold of yourself!" Sally exclaimed. "Princess Esterhazy and Countess Lieven were in her box!"

"Foreigners, of course. *They* look at things quite differently, I assure you!" Julia said with a truly English worldview.

"They are Patronesses of Almack's! Surely you cannot be more respectable than that! Lady Rockhall seems quite respectable, I assure you! And she and Tilghman barely spoke three words to each other! It was the merest politeness! She moves in very high diplomatic circles. She was an ambassadress and besides, she's old! Why, she must be *forty*!" Sally finished naively.

"Ancient!" agreed her sister vehemently, and began to sob. "Oh, Sally, I am *so* unhappy!"

Sally slipped an arm around her sister comfortingly. "There, there, dear one, I am here!" she said soothingly. "You cannot possibly believe Tilghman is in love with that old hag?" Privately, she had a feeling the soigné Lady Rockhall might not appreciate being called an old hag, but her aim at that moment was to comfort her sister.

Sally said, "Oh, Julia, you can't possibly believe he's playing you false with Lady Rockhall!"

"I think he is, and so does Alex," Julia sniffled into her handkerchief. "They are such particular friends! And she is knowledgeable, and intelligent, and educated, and she has spent her whole life in the Foreign Office! Her father and her late husband were both ambassadors and diplomats. She's even supposed to have been a great friend of the Tsar! Tilghman talks to her about all the things I don't understand! Why wouldn't he turn to her when he discovered what a great mistake it was to marry me? Besides," she added in an awful voice, "Old Lady Tilghman thinks she's wonderful! She never loses an opportunity to tell me so!"

"But Tilghman married *you*, Julia," Sally pointed out. "He married you because he loved you and you loved him!"

"*I* loved *him*," Julia voiced in tragic accents. "*He* married *me* because he needed an heir. And I can't even seem to do that!" This melancholy thought seemed to drive her into deeper misery, for she burst into a round of new sobs. "And now that we're not even speaking . . . well you can just imagine how well *that* is going! I am the most miserable wretch alive!"

"He did not tell you that was why he married you, did he?" Sally asked.

"He didn't have to! I can see the disappointment in the way he looks at me! And I am a miserable failure as a hostess, too! My French is atrocious, and I have no head for politics or diplomacy or any of the things Important People like to talk about, and I know he is deeply disappointed in me! He barely comes home! He spends all his time at the Foreign Office!"

"So would I, if my house were perpetually in a state of uproar and remodeling," Sally said with a great deal of common sense. "You know, you really ought to say enough and bring that all to a close. I nearly fell into a bucket of paint this morning on my way to the breakfast room."

"But Tilghman wants the house re-done. Besides, as long as it's in an uproar, I don't have to entertain Important People. They make me feel quite stupid."

"You are not stupid, Jules, just awfully thick sometimes! And don't look at me that way, because it's true. When we were in schoolroom, you could run circles around me in any subject when you put your mind to it! But you never put your mind to it, because no one expected you to! Because you are the Beauty of the family, and everyone . . . including you . . . expects you can get through life on your looks alone!"

This observation was enough to bring Julia up short. She stared at her sister in amazement. "Where did you come up with that idea?" she asked.

"I have had nothing to do for the past year at home but think. It's true, you know. Besides, I think Will had the idea. He says beauty is its own reason for existing, but when one is a *jolie laide* like me, one should develop one's mind."

The Blythes were not a family given to deep introspection, but Julia, digesting her sister's observations, had to nod. "Alex has become my only true friend, you know! He *understands*!" She broke into fresh weeping, digging for her handkerchief in her reticule. "When he came back to town, he saw how cast down I was, and how lonely, he made such an effort to make sure that I was going out and meeting people with whom I could have some entertainment, interesting people, not in the least bit stuffy or frightening!"

"Oh, Alex is wonderful, isn't he?" Sally enthused, happy for any opportunity to talk about him.

"He is most entertaining," Julia replied. "But, I assure you, it is only a friendship! Unlike Tilghman's relationship with Lady Rockhall!" she added bitterly.

"Oh, Julia, I don't think it's that way at all," Sally replied, although she was uncertain whether she was speaking of her sister and Alex or Tilghman and Lady Rockhall. "What does Alex say?"

"I would never discuss it with him," Julia said stiffly. "Oh, Sally, I would die before I would let anyone know how miserable I am! I daresay in time I shall learn not to care!"

Quite used to Julia's histrionics, generally founded upon little more than moonbeams and a highly developed sense of drama, Sally nonetheless felt the need to put her arms around her sister and comfort her.

"I'll tell you what we both need! We'll go to

Gunter's and have an ice! That will make you feel much better! Then we'll go to the Pantheon Bazaar and shop for bargains! You never could resist a bargain!"

Julia smiled and hugged Sally, all the while dabbing at her eyes. "You are the dearest of sisters," she said. "Here I am going on about my troubles, and this should be the happiest time of your life. Tell me how—"

"Oh, it was nothing really. We just agreed on becoming engaged," Sally said vaguely. Her own problems seemed quite insignificant compared to those of her sister. But she somehow did not like the idea of Alex being involved in all of this. Why, she was hard pressed to say. But the feeling would not go away.

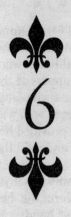

It was two days before Mr. Starret bethought himself of calling upon his fiancée. From the moment he had returned to the bachelor digs he shared with the Honorable Barnaby Tennant and Mr. Frank Holmes in the Albany, he had pretty much forgotten about Sally, his attention immediately being claimed by such interesting matters as a horse auction at Tattersall's, a boxing match held in the village of Kensington, and a cockfight in the East End. There were Brooks & Watiers to be looked in upon, and Scott to be visited for some new raiment. And of course, the charms of the lovely actress Kathleen Quinn.

Since Miss Quinn had many, many other admirers, including Barney and Frank, Will was fairly safe from any entanglement more complex than being one of her entourage for an after-theater supper.

Perhaps because the commonsensical Miss Quinn sensed no threat to her virtue could come from a trio of sports-minded lads, Will, Barney, and Frank were favored to escort her to after-theater suppers at the Cole Hole, Vauxhall Gardens, and other such places of entertainment. Keenly sensed, but never seen was another, more amorous gentleman who provided her with elegant finery, handsome jewels, and paid the rent on her luxurious quarters on Half Moon Street. All attempts by his jealous rivals to identify this mysterious lover had so far met with failure, but her dresser hinted strongly that he was most handsome and fashionable and evidently, very wealthy, for he was very free with his blunt. This last was of prime importance to Miss Quinn, a pragmatist, who realized she must gather her rosebuds while she might, and invest them where she could assure herself of a good return for her lonely old age.

It was in hopes of impressing Miss Quinn that Will found his way into Hamlet's, one of the city's finest jewelers. Baubles, he had noticed, seemed to evoke a most grateful response from the actress, and the larger the bauble, the more grateful her response. He was inspecting a velvet tray of turquoise and diamond pieces when he felt a tap on his shoulder and looked up to see Alex smiling down at him.

"Purchasing an engagement present?" Alex asked. He surveyed the tray of jewelry with a knowing eye. "Turquoises may be all the crack right now in theatrical circles, but I'd say they were a little common for Sally. She's a female made for pearls, I've noticed."

At that moment, Will realized that he disliked Alex intensely. And it wasn't just his cologne. It was his attitude of superiority that rankled, the way he never seemed to have a hair out of place but seemed to look down on anyone who might. Since Alex had also put him in mind that custom dictated he give Sally some token as an engagement present, Will was very annoyed indeed. That Alex was correct, and pearls were perfect for Sally only added to the fire.

"I was thinking amethysts," Will said, somewhat sullenly.

Alex made a tsking sound. "Oh, my dear boy, *never* amethysts with red hair, don't you know. You know, one would have thought to have seen you hauntin' Tilghman House, being engaged and all. If you don't watch it, you might find someone's stepped on your toes."

He plucked an invisible spot of lint from Will's lapel. "That is, if you really are engaged," he added with his annoying smile.

"Of course we're engaged, why shouldn't we be?" Will asked irritably.

"Oh, I don't know. You don't seem like a couple smelling of April and May. Sally is sometimes so easy to read, just like an open book. Why, I almost feel inclined to think she wants me to be jealous," Alex said softly. "Females are such intriguing creatures, don't you think?"

Before Will had to reply, Mr. Hamlet himself emerged from the nether regions of the store. "I have had a chance to appraise that necklace, Mr. Quartermaine, and while the value of rubies is just now somewhat depressed, I think I may be able to offer you a good price," he said.

Alex bowed toward Will. "Perhaps I will see you at Almack's tonight," he said. "Miss Blythe has already favored me with the promise of a waltz!"

Will turned back to the clerk. He pointed to a turquoise bracelet. "I've changed my mind about the turquoises. I'd like to see your pearls, if you please!"

Damme Alex Quartermaine! he thought.

When Mr. Starret was shown into Tilghman House, he found Sally coming down the stairs. At first, he thought she was Julia, for she was much changed since the last time he had seen her. Her hair was cropped into a profusion of curls that framed her face, and she was wearing a high crowned bonnet trimmed with tartan ribbons that set her face off to great advantage. She was wearing a walking dress of dark fawn Circassian cloth, with a square standing collar and wadded bands down the front and carrying a cashmere shawl over one arm. For a moment, he was unable to speak, merely thrust a wrapped and ribboned box toward her.

"Will!" she cried, surprised. She accepted the box from him, and broke into a smile. "Oh, Will, a present? For me? I was going to scold you for not coming around, but I will forgive you now!"

He nodded and watched as she opened the box and withdrew a long string of large, lustrous pearls.

Sally gasped. "Oh, Will! You shouldn't!" she exclaimed. "They're so beautiful!" Impulsively, she stood on tiptoe and kissed him. Before he knew what he was doing, he had wrapped her in his arms.

"Of course he should," said Julia, standing at the top of the stairs and admiring this pretty scene. "Those are lovely pearls, Will! What a superb engagement gift!"

As if they had been burned, Will and Sally drew apart, neither one knowing where to look.

"But I can't let you—that wouldn't be fair! Oh, Will!" Sally exclaimed. "You are the dearest and kindest of friends—of fiancés!"

"Nonsense," he said gruffly. "Wanted you to have them. Thought you would look very pretty in pearls."

"And so she does," Julia said, relieving her sister of the necklace and holding it up to herself as she looked in the great carved and gilded hall mirror. "What a romantic gift! Oh, Sally, you must let me borrow them for the opera some night!"

"Nonsense, Jules," Will teased her, "You've probably got cabinets full of jewelry. Sally, doesn't . . . yet."

Miss Blythe threw him a speaking look, but he merely shrugged and smiled.

"Well, have you come to ravish Sally away from me? I was going to force her to go for a nice brisk walk with me to see the dowager, but since you are here, I suppose I can get Pomfret to accompany me to Grosvenor Square. I daresay that you two would like some time alone. And I'm sure that Sally would do anything to avoid seeing my mama-in-law. *I* would, but alas I have no excuse!"

"I was hoping Sally might come up and ride with

me around the park," Will admitted, seeing the imploring look in her eyes giving way to an expression of vast relief at being spared an afternoon of the dowager's disapproval.

"Very well!" Julia replied, tapping Will on the sleeve with her gloves. "But I warn you, before you leave town, you will have to pay a courtesy call on her, the pair of you!"

"I shall wear my new pearls on the outside of my pelisse, so everyone can see them," Sally said, suiting her actions to her words.

"Oh, Will," Sally said as he handed her up into the phaeton, "I am *so* particularly glad to see you!"

Her companion, taking the reins up in his hands and advising his groom that he would meet back here in a couple of hours, looked both guilty and gratified. "Sorry I haven't been by before! Thought you might be busy with Alex. Then it occurred to me that it might look strange if I didn't put in an appearance at Tilghman House! Supposed to be engaged! People might start to talk, you know."

He nodded. "Thought you might put my head out for washing for neglecting you," he added.

"Will, you shouldn't have gone out and bought pearls, although they are lovely," Sally said, placing her hand on his. "I feel so guilty now!"

"Thought you might like them, pearls suit you, you know," Will said, pleased with himself. It was on the tip of his tongue to tell her about his encounter with Alex, but for some reason, he was unable to define, he kept silent on that head, saying instead, "That is, we're engaged, have to get

you an engagement present. Thing to do! People
expect it."

"I shall return them to you the minute this all
over, I promise! Will, it's far too much money to
spend on a Banbury tale! You are the dearest of
friends to go this far, and I am the greatest wretch
alive for dragging you into this!"

"No need to do that," Will said. "Not as if I can't
stand the blunt, you know. And recall, Sally, I
agreed to this!"

"Yes, but—" Sally broke off. She bit her lower
lip and fingered the pearls.

"Cold feet?" Will asked her. "Or is Alex not taking the bait?" This last question, he knew, would
break her mood. And to that end, he was willing to
provoke one of their rows, perhaps because he was
not comfortable with the direction the conversation was taking.

"Trouble with Alex? Not coming up to snuff?" he
asked again when she did not immediately respond.

"Well, that, too," Sally admitted. "But it's Tilghman and Julia!"

A muscle in Will's jaw flexed. "Oh?" he responded,
suddenly concentrating on his team. It was on the
tip of his tongue to tell her that affairs between
married people were a forbidden area, but he
regarded Julia much in the light of a sister and was
sincerely fond of Tilghman.

"Will, they're barely speaking to each other!"

"All married couples have tiffs, daresay it's a
part of the fun. M'sister Louisa says making up a
fight is wonderful."

Sally twisted her pearls between her gloves fingers. "I can't help but feel this is much deeper than a mere tiff," she said, and told Will about Julia's suspicions.

Will listened intently until she had finished, then whistled. "Lady Rockhall, hey? Well, if it's so . . . and I don't say it is, because you never know . . . Tilghman's got good taste, you must admit that! But if Julia don't watch it, she *will* catch cold! Alex Quartermaine runs with a damned fast crowd!"

"I knew you would see the worst in Alex!" Sally said sharply, quite forgetting her new pearls. "Alex is too much of a gentleman to *ever*—"

"I tell you, Sally, whatever's goin' on, stay out of it!" Will advised her bluntly. "If you try to meddle in this, you *will* catch cold!"

"But—"

"I said no, and I meant it, Sally!" Will exclaimed, forgetting his fashionable drawl. "No good whatsoever can come from meddling between Julia and Tilghman! Whatever is going on, you can only make it worse!" He frowned. "You—we're in deep enough as it is, between the two of us, with this tangle! Besides," he added in a more reasonable tone of voice, "I can't imagine anyone as top-lofty as Tilghman havin' an affair! You know what a high stickler he is! Trust me, this is one of Julia's flights!"

Sally looked up at Will. "Oh, are you certain?" she asked hopefully.

"No," Will said after some reflection. "Fella could appear to be as sober as a Methodist and have a secret wild streak. Of course, it's hard to imagine a Public Man like Tilghman having a wild streak. Or a secret life, either. Where would he find the time? Always working out trade agreements and treaties and such. I would think that would be very time consuming, wouldn't you?"

"You would think so," Sally agreed. "But you never know! But, it is so horrid to see Julia pretending she's happy when she is not! Will, what shall I do?"

"Nothing," Will replied. "I can guarantee you this, Sally. If you meddle in Julia and Tilghman's affairs, it will make our little secret look like the merest trifle! But I still cannot like Alex's involvement!"

"You *would* say that! Why, you don't even *know* Alex!" Sally rose hotly in Mr. Quartermaine's defense. "He's only trying to help her because she's my sister, I'm sure!"

"And has he been hanging around since you came into town?"

"He called upon us yesterday," Sally said coldly, "And he will be escorting us to Almack's tonight. A place, I might add, you said you would rather not go!"

"Better him than me," Will said firmly.

Almack's Assembly Rooms, located on King Street, St. James's, was, for aspirants to the highest ton, the closest thing to heaven on earth.

To receive a voucher from one of the Assembly's Patronesses was to be assured that one had entered the highest levels of society. And these vouchers were not easy to procure, for they could only be issued by the Patronesses, a group of ladies who ruled London Society with a collective whim of iron.

Will Starret might find Almack's dull, as did many other young men on the town, but even he had breathed sigh of relief when Lady Sefton, a friend of his mother's had sent him a voucher in his first year on the town. For either Julia or Sally, to fail to receive a voucher would have been a serious setback indeed.

The voucher, once issued, allowed its owner to dress in his most formal knee britches or her best ball gown and purchase a ticket of admission from the majordomo, the redoubtable Mr. Willis. Once inside the cavernous, somewhat shabbily furnished rooms, one could dance to the orchestra led by the violinist Mr. Gowe, play whist for silver stakes in the card rooms, eat an indifferent meal in the supper rooms, and, if one were thirsty, drink lemonade or punch, the only beverages served. And of these two, many preferred the lemonade.

One could only waltz with the permission of one or another of the Patronesses, and only dance two dances with the same person in the course of the night. Heaven help the person who violated these or any of the many other rules of conduct laid down by the Patronesses! Promptly at eleven o'clock, Mr. Willis closed the doors. Not even the Duke of Wellington was admitted after that magic hour.

Fortunately for Mr. Quartermaine, the Patronesses, like so many other females, looked upon him with favor. There had never been any question of issuing him a voucher, no matter what vague rumors had swirled about his handsome head. His birth was respectable, his manners impeccable, his ton unimpeachable. With so many young bachelors more interested in finding their pleasure in other, more interesting places, he was considered, in spite of his rumored lack of fortune, to be a prize.

Sally could not help but note how the ladies, even the haughty Mrs. Drummond Burrell smiled upon Alex when he made his entrance with a Blythe sister on each arm. Lady Tilghman was immediately surrounded by a court of her admirers, who alternately demanded a dance or begged her to come and enliven a game or two of silver loo. Since this was Sally's first public appearance since her return to town, it was not long before her friends claimed her, too, and several men were quick to scribble their names into her dance card. But not before Alex, with a flourish, took the card and signed his own name for the first waltz.

It would have been impossible for her not to notice the envious looks she received when Alex led her out on the floor, and Sally was vain enough to enjoy this immensely. It was the first chance she had to speak to him alone.

As he whirled her lightly around the floor, he smiled down at her beneath his lashes. "You look ravishing tonight, Sally," he said.

She smiled with pleasure, knowing that she did look very well in an ivory silk ball gown, under a half skirt of blond lace, trimmed with appliquéed satin cockleshells and sea horses. And of course, she wore her new pearls. Now, perhaps he would begin to regret not paying more attention to her, she thought!

"I might say the same of you," she replied aloud.

"Then we must be the handsomest couple on the floor," Alex remarked airily. "And the envy of all."

He seemed content to dance in silence for what seemed to Sally to be a very long time, only smiling down at her in his way, as if he knew that she had a hundred questions for him that she could not ask.

"New pearls?" he asked at last.

"You noticed," Sally said. "How like you to notice something like a new piece of jewelry! They were a gift."

"An engagement present, perhaps?"

There was something like a whisper of mockery in his voice. Sally glanced up at him, aware color was flaming into her cheeks.

"They were from Will. An engagement present. He is so thoughtful."

"Touché!" Alex said regretfully. "I suppose I deserved that! Or *did* the better man win?"

"I'm sure I don't know what you mean, Alex."

"Don't you?"

"Where have you been, Alex?" Sally looked up at him, seriously. "You left town shortly after I did, with never a word."

"Oh, I had my reasons for leaving," he answered lightly. "And I suppose I was bit remiss in not getting in touch with you. But, it never occurred to me that you would care."

"Of course I care . . . cared," she amended quickly, adding, "I thought that we were friends!"

"And I thought that we were so much more than just friends." Alex spun her around the floor. She was helpless, under his control in his arms. "But you, alas, seem to have chosen another."

Sally found nothing that she could reply to this. Of course, looking into those beautiful eyes, she wanted to tell him all, spill out the truth, but she could not. No properly brought up young lady could.

"Unless . . ." Alex whispered the teasing word into her ear.

She glanced up at him, waiting for him to finish his thought, her heart beating fiercely.

"Ah, but what's the use of wondering?" he sighed. "You have quite dashed my hopes, Sally. I suppose I shall have to wear the willow."

At that very moment, the dance ended. After applauding politely, he led Sally back to her seat.

He did not, she thought, appear to be wearing the willow as he went to claim another pretty female as his partner in the quadrille. As young Viscount Forley claimed her hand, she followed him out to the floor. From across the room, Alex threw her a yearning glance, as if to say that he would much prefer to partner Sally to the lovely Miss Yarrow.

Later in the evening, when Julia reappeared from the card rooms, complaining somewhat sullenly about her losses, saying she had a headache and wanted to go home, Sally was more than happy to leave without protest. She had things she needed to ponder alone.

7

When Sally came down to breakfast the next morning, she found Tilghman, as usual, buried beneath a stack of red dispatch boxes, reading documents as he ate and drank his coffee. The smell of fresh plaster hung in the air, and a cheerful young man in a smock was installing new cornice and swag moldings in the hall, whistling "Over the Hills and Far Away" as he worked.

After accepting a muted grunt from her brother-in-law as his customary breakfast greeting—experience had taught her that he was *not* a morning person—she went to the sideboard and helped herself to eggs, marmalade, ham, and toast, then sat at her own place to scan the newspapers as she poured her coffee.

The morning mail had been delivered, and a small stack of gilt-edged invitations and letters sat

beside her place at table. After she had glanced
through the newspapers, she began thumb through
the letters and was pursuing a crossed note from
her mother with all the news from home when the
butler announced that there was a person request-
ing to see my lord.

"I placed him in your study, sir," Tilghman was
informed, "there being no workmen there this
morning."

Tilghman raised an eyebrow. After excusing himself, he left the table.

In a short while, he was back, looking very grim
indeed. Without preamble, he placed a velvet box
on the table in front of Sally and opened it.

"Do you know anything about this?" he asked.

Sally looked down at a necklace of *tremblant*
rubies and diamonds shaped into tiny flowers
and butterflies set into huge castings of white
gold. It was as bulky and old-fashioned as her
engagement ring, the Rococo design of the past
century.

"No," she answered, completely at a loss.

"Nothing?" Tilghman asked in a awful voice.

Sally looked up at him, shaking her head. His
eyes flashed darkly and his lips were set in a thin
line. She had never seem Tilghman angry before,
and she drew back a little.

"I'll have an explanation for this or know the reason why!" he exclaimed. He scooped up the necklace and turning on his heel, started angrily out of
the room.

Just as he was about to open the door, it was

opened from the other side and Julia, wearing a new and very ornate morning dress of ivory jaconet muslin trimmed with a great many ruffles and easings came into the room. "Good morning," she said cheerfully, and indeed, she looked much more the thing than she had since Sally's arrival.

"Sit down, ma'am," Tilghman said in the same awful voice, closing the door behind her.

Obviously stunned, Julia sank into a chair.

Tilghman seemed to be oblivious to Sally's presence, so great was his rage as he dangled the necklace in front of her.

Julia gasped, made an effort to snatch it away from him, but Tilghman was too quick for her. He dropped it into her lap. "I would like an explanation, ma'am," he said icily.

Julia was very white, but determined to brazen it out. "I don't know what you mean, Tilghman," she said, but her voice quivered.

"I mean, my dear, that not half an hour ago, I received a visit from Mr. Hamlet, of Hamlet's, the Bond Street jewelers. He, oh, ever so tactfully, so much the gentleman . . . suggested that I might like to purchase this back. It seems one of his clerks bought it from a person who came in a few days ago. I believe the word is *pawned*. The person *pawned* this . . . trinket . . . for a few hundred pounds. Naturally Mr. Hamlet recognized the Tilghman Rubies . . . what jeweler in London wouldn't? . . . and quite naturally wished to know if I wanted to purchase them back! Oh, it was all very discreet, I assure you! Thank God that our family has been doing business with Hamlet's for years! If you've drawn the bustle, that's one thing, ma'am! But to try to sell the most famous Tilghman family heirloom in existence is quite another! They are not yours to pawn, but belong to the family, as they have for generations!"

Julia looked quite distraught. Drained of color, her face was paler than her gown. She wrung her hands and licked her lips. Her eyes darted around the room.

Sally, watching all of this, felt trapped. If she could have discreetly slipped out the door, she would have done so. There was nothing she wanted less than to be trapped in this family quarrel. Still, she could not believe that even dear, scatterbrained Julia would have done something this foolish. And why? Tilghman paid her a handsome allowance, and she had her own funds from her settlement. Sally knew that Tilghman's man of business paid her extravagant dress bills regularly. Something else was going on here, and she was not quite sure what it was. Could it be that Julia was keeping secrets, even from her?

Guiltily, she reflected on her own secret.

But, Julia stood up, drawing herself up to her full height. Color flooded into her pale cheeks and her eyes flashed as she confronted her husband, eye to cyc.

"A fine thing that you should talk to me about Tilghman Family Tradition!" she flared. "What about you and your dear friend Lady Rockhall? What did you purchase for her from Mr. Hamlet?"

"What?" Tilghman asked. He had not been expecting a counterattack.

"You can give that dowdy old piece back to your mother! Doubtless she hasn't given you a moment's peace since you asked for all the dreary old Tilghman Family pieces! For your information, my lord, there must have been some sort of misunderstanding! I . . . I sent that necklace to be cleaned, not pawned!"

And with that, she swept out of the room with as much dignity as she could muster. After a second, there was the distant sound of her bedchamber door slamming shut.

The young plasterer in the hall whistled through his teeth as she swept past him and pretended great concentration on a daub fruit basket he was just then applying to the wall. It was the only sound in the house, which had suddenly become very silent indeed.

Tilghman looked down at the necklace, which he was crumbling in his fist. As he opened his hand, the jewels spilled out across the table, sadly bent on their stalks.

"Hellfire and damnation!" he exclaimed to no one in particular. "Can't a man have a bit of peace in his own house? Do I have to live at my damned club?" With that, he swept up the papers and the dispatch boxes and slammed out of the room and down the hall.

Sally only hoped the coachman was waiting for him outside the door.

She was about to follow her sister up the stairs for a long, searching conference when the butler appeared again. "Mr. Quartermaine is in the Blue Drawing Room, Miss," he announced. "He wishes to speak with you. I informed him that my lady was not receiving callers," he added with a discreet cough.

There was nothing for it, Sally realized, but that she must go to him at once. She would have been less than human had she not felt a thrill of anticipation at seeing him.

When she entered the room, Alex, outfitted splendidly in riding attire was gazing at his reflection in the mirror. When he was sure that he was impeccable, from the top of his burnished raven locks to the toes of his gleaming top boots, he turned to smile at her, offering her his hands. "Ah, I thought that I would go riding this morning, and that I would drop by and see if you and Julia wanted to come. But the butler tells me she is indisposed, so I suppose will have to be you and me. How soon can you be ready?"

Fortunately for anyone else who might have desired her company, Sally had no other engagement that morning. "Fifteen minutes!" she said. "And I have something I most particularly need to seek your advice upon!" she added.

Pausing only to ask a footman to see that the mare Tilghman kept for the convenience of his guests was saddled and waiting for her, Sally ran up the stairs. She paused only briefly before her sister's door, then ran down the hallway to her own room without knocking.

Within a half an hour, she was riding along Rotten Row beside Alex, looking, she hoped, very handsome in her slate-colored bombazine habit, trimmed with braid and finished with a mannish stock at the throat. Upon her coppery curls she had placed a black beaver topper with a single plume that swept her cheek. The mare was fresh, but no real challenge to Sally's equestrienne skill, which, she reflected, was just as well, since she most particularly wanted no distractions this morning.

Alex himself was distracting enough; mounted on a rather showy Arabian gelding, he nodded and tipped his high-crowned beaver to almost every fashionable lady they passed. And the ladies in turn smiled upon him, stopping them every few yards for a moment of conversation. For some of them, it was almost all they could do to include Sally.

It was only when they had turned off on one of the bridal paths that Sally was able to tell him about events of the morning. "I only tell you," she finished naively, "because I know that you are Julia's cicisbeo in chief, and that you have her best interests at heart!"

Alex looked over at her from beneath his lashes. "Why don't you confide these things to Will Starret? He is, after all, your fiancé, is he not?" he asked.

Sally frowned uncertainly. It was not the reply she had wanted or expected from him. "Because," she said baldly, "Will says that he absolutely refuses to become involved in the quarrels between a man and his wife, and that I should not either. But Julia is my sister, and I am naturally concerned. And I thought that you would be, too, and that you would know what to do!"

Alex replied with a laugh. "Will is not quite as blockheaded as I thought!"

"Will is extremely intelligent!" Sally replied defensively.

Alex tapped her gently on the shoulder with his riding crop. "Thank you for telling me these things. I shall attempt to discover if there is anything you can do."

"But do you know if Julia tried to sell the Tilghman Rubies? And if she did, why? Alex, there is something going on that Julia won't tell me about."

"Perhaps she doesn't think you need to know," he replied. "And frankly, Sally, I think you would be the better not to press her for answers. It could be very uncomfortable, you know." He reached out and caressed her cheek with a gloved hand. "It's much too fine a day to be thinking about other people's problems. Let's talk about you and me."

Sally swallowed hard. Alex's dark, hooded eyes held hers for a long moment and his mocking smile curled his lip. Lightly, ever so lightly, his fingers traced the curve of her cheekbone.

Sally felt as if she were mesmerized. She closed her eyes and leaned slightly toward him, her lips parted. She could smell his cologne, a musky male scent that hung on the crisp morning air. She heard his saddle leather creak as he leaned toward her.

"Hullo, you two! Wait up!"

The sound of hoof beats cut through the moment like a knife. Sally turned to see three young horsemen bearing down on them at a canter. Alex made a sound under his breath that might have been a frustrated curse.

"Good morning!" Will addressed them, slowing his big bay to draw up beside them on the path. The Honorable Barnaby Tennant and Mr. Frank Holmes drew up on the other side, effectively surrounding them.

"Sally, fancy running into you here!" Will said, frowning at her. "Shouldn't go off the Row unescorted! Not the thing to do you know!" He leaned over and gave her a small, dry peck on the cheek. "Alex," he said, acknowledging the other man's presence with a nod.

In ordinary times, Sally would have been quite happy to see Barney and Frank, for they formed a part of her court and were men she had known since childhood, being Will's best friends. Barney was stocky and round, with a blond, childlike countenance, while Frank's saturnine, funereal aspect complemented his tall, stringy frame and belied a most jovial temperament.

"Here's a stroke, my boys! Quartermaine! He could take a fourth share!" Barney exclaimed after greeting Sally. "Oh, and congratulations, Sally! . . . Know you and Will will do the happy!" he added as an afterthought.

"Oh, yes! Offer felicitations, Sally! Look forward to dancing at your wedding! Promised Will we wouldn't pull any tricks like tying old shoes to the wedding coach or chivareeing you!"

"I'm so grateful!" Sally managed to murmur. She turned to glare at Will, but he only stared back at her with blank, impassive eyes, raising one shoulder in a shrug.

"Thing of it is, old man," continued Barney, feeling more pressing business than Will's wedding was to hand. "We've taken a lodge in Hants for hunting. Need a fourth. Overshire had to drop out when his regiment was transferred to Tunbridge Wells. Thought you might be interested." Actually anyone male with forty guineas to put to the Season's lease would have been welcomed at this late date. Mr. Quartermaine was simply the first eligible gentleman they had encountered.

"Fine country," Frank added. "Old Adderwell's pack! And there's a bit of shooting to go on, too!"

"We need a fourth man to make the share," Barney said. "Think you'd be interested?"

Sally shot Will a burning look, but he only shrugged. A share was, after all, a share, and this was man's business.

"That sounds good," Alex agreed. "By October, I can always use a repairing lease! How is the shooting?"

Infuriated, Sally watched as Alex, Barney, and Frank fell into an entirely masculine discussion of guns, shot, bags, and other hunting things.

"How could you?" she demanded under her breath as she turned toward Will. "Just when he was about to—"

"Kiss you?" Will returned in the same undertone. "Have a little common sense, Sally! Suppose someone else, someone like Lady Jersey or the Dowager had come up that path! That would have been a pretty scandal for all of London to hear! Engaged to someone else, and found kissin' Alex

Quartermaine on a bridal path in the park! Especially," he added in injured tones, "if that someone is me! How do you think it makes me look? Like a damned fool, that's how!"

"Well, I still think you could have been a little more . . . tactful!" Sally shot back. "Hunting lodge! You men are all alike!"

"If this weren't a public place, I'd—" Will hissed.

"You'd what? Do something Gothick?"

Sensing something amiss, Sally and Will suddenly broke off to find Alex, Barney, and Frank all staring at them.

"Well!" Will said, recovering himself quickly. "For my part, I don't care if we have the honeymoon in Scotland or Wales. Chose whatever you like."

If Sally had not been so excessively angry with Will at that moment, she would have applauded his quick thinking.

"Cross crabs, are we?" Alex asked in a teasing voice when they had separated from the gentlemen and were walking down the path toward the Row.

"Will is very jealous," Sally replied airily.

"He has much to be jealous of!" Alex replied. "You and I, Miss Blythe are going to have a tête à tête—not today, but very soon!" He smiled. "In the meantime, don't worry yourself about Julia! I shall have everything under control, I promise you." He stroked her cheek again. "And, my dear Sally, I think it would be better if you and I pretended that this conversation never took place, at least as far as Julia is concerned. You know that she fancies herself a complete hand!"

"A very grand cake I should make of myself if I went prattling to Julia," Sally cried. "But Alex, do you know what is plaguing her? Please tell me if you do. I am her sister, and it must always be my concern to help her, just as she would help me!"

Alex shrugged. "Some things a young lady is not equipped to deal with, and this must needs be one of them," he said smoothly. "Trust me. I have been on the town longer than you, and of course, I must hold Julia's best interests at heart myself. As you say, I am her cicisbeo in chief. And now, my dear, it is entirely too late, and I should be getting you back to Tilghman House. We must ride again soon."

It was typical of Alex that he offered nothing more than a vague promise, Sally thought with just a twinge of annoyance. She immediately felt guilty for being annoyed at such a nonpareil and applied herself to trusting Mr. Quartermaine all the way home.

When Sally returned to Upper Mount Street, she found Julia prostrate on her chaise with the redoubtable Pomfret bathing her temples in hartshorn and water while Betty somewhat ineffectually flourished a brandy decanter and a glass hovering nearby and emitting small, concerned sounds.

"So you went for a ride with Alex," Julia said thickly, glaring at her sister. "While I lie here, prostrate with anxiety! I might have known you would think of yourself first!"

It was clear to Sally that Julia was in a mood to pick a quarrel, whether the servants were present

or not. Since a great part of her reason for leaving
with Alex had been to avoid just such a scene as
Julia was prone to enact, her sister quickly made an
exit.

She knew Julia's method, when caught doing
something questionable, was to take the offensive.
And, she thought, pawning the Tilghman Rubies
was something that could be classified as questionable. Or worse. Julia was capable of some scatterbrained acts, but this had to the worst one so far,
Sally thought as she stripped out of her riding habit.

In fact, she thought, unbraiding her hair and
pulling the brush through her tangled curls, pawning the Tilghman Rubies seemed much worse than
pretending to be engaged.

Or, at least about the same. She looked at herself
in the mirror and saw a young lady with problems.
Hopefully, Alex could discover precisely why Julia
had sold a family heirloom. It simply made no sense.

By afternoon, Julia still remained cloistered in
her room with Pomfret and Betty both in attendance. It was not that Sally minded drawing her
own bath and doing her own hair, for she had been
used to doing so ever since she had been in the
schoolroom, but she did mind, and very much,
when the Dowager Lady Tilghman paid a call and
Julia remained indisposed, forcing her to deal with
the Dowager alone.

Aurora, Dowager Countess Tilghman was as
gray and hard as stone, from the thin set of her lips
to her grizzled hair to the perennial shades of half-
mourning she had adapted fifteen years before on

the death of her spouse. Even the large and dingy
diamond rings she displayed on thin, twig-like
hands were gray. She came accompanied by her
companion, a colorless distant cousin of indeter-
minate age known in the family as Cousin Pansy
Beaufort, whom the Dowager bullied mercilessly.
Indeed, there was nothing more the Dowager
enjoyed than ordering people about ruthlessly,
unless it was those who were in no way intimidated
by her. The Dowager's constant accessory was her
ebony silver-headed cane, which she used more for
conversational emphasis then support.

Having seated herself in the Blue Drawing Room,
she ordered Cousin Pansy Beaufort to stop lolly-
gagging about and sit down. She then swept a knowledgeable eye over Sally's toilette and hair, mentally
estimating the cost down to the last half penny. She
shook her head over the decor of the room, deploring
the utter depravity of modern taste. Only then did
she proceed to her reason for the unexpected pleasure of her company.

"Won't come out of her room will she?" the
Dowager said with grim satisfaction as Sally
informed her that Julia was not feeling all the thing.
"Small wonder! But it won't do, you know! The latest on-dit is that my son is talking about moving to
his club. Is that true?"

Sally shrugged. "You'd have to ask him, ma'am.
I am not in his confidence."

The Dowager looked at her with small, dark
eyes. She looked, Julia thought, rather like a parrot,
an ill-tempered gray parrot.

"I understand you're engaged to young Will Starret," the Dowager said with the sudden delivery of a twenty-one pounder opening fire on an unsuspecting merchant man. "What happened to that Quartermaine lad, the one who was so particular to you last Season?"

"You mean Venetia Waycross' son?" Cousin Pansy asked timorously.

"Now who else would it be?" the Dowager said in heavy tones, and Miss Beaufort sank back into her chair and the silence that was her habit, looking very much like a dormouse.

"His mother was a Waycross, now that I come to think on it. Perfectly respectable family, but the Quartermaines were always a ramshackle group! I remember his grandfather perfectly well. A handsome man, but not steady! Not steady at all! After he died, his mother raised him, you know. Alexander, I mean! Looks just like his grandfather. As far as Venetia was concerned, he could do no wrong, gave him his head on everything. Very bad way to raise children! William Starret, on the other hand, is from very good blood on both sides. *His* mother was a Downe! No skeletons in *their* closets!"

"What do you mean, ma'am?" Sally asked curiously.

"Just what I said, Miss Blythe! I say what I mean and I mean what I say! Can't stand the mealy-mouthed way people go on these days! There was bad blood in the Quartermaines! Always was, always will be! That young Starret is a good choice! He'll make a fine husband! A good family, very respectable people! Is that your engagement ring? Let me see it, child."

Dutifully, Sally presented her hand for the Dowager's scrutiny. Those who said the old lady had lost her facilities were dead wrong. The Dowager might be old, but she was sharp. She examined the ring through her quizzing glass and nodded her approval. "First water, that stone! And a fine, substantial setting, too! None of this wispy modern stuff! The Tilghmans own some very fine pieces, too, you know! Why, the Tilghman Rubies are quite historical, you know! Ought to be in a museum, but your sister don't seem to like them. Can't say I blame her, really. Rubies don't suit that yaller hair of hers."

Sally threw the Dowager a sharp look, but said nothing.

Eventually, the older woman rose to take her leave, sending cousin Cousin Pansy out to inform the butler she would want her carriage.

As she was drawing on her gloves, she frowned at Sally. "I daresay everyone thinks I'm an old gorgon, and I daresay I am! It's one of the few privileges of age, my dear, as you will find out someday, to say exactly what you think and do as you please! But I cannot like hearing that my son and his wife are on the outs! Julia's young yet, she hasn't learned the ways of the world. And I ain't sayin' I raised a perfect son! Too much like his father, may he rest in peace! But Julia could be a help to him, the way I was to my Augustus, if she'd just put one half the effort into the business that she does jaunting around town with

that set of Alexander Quartermaine's! When you
marry a Public Man, you become a Public Woman,
and you do twice as much behind the scenes, giving
dinners holding evenings, really talking to people, as
he does in all the diplomatic receptions! You'd be
amazed how many agreements and accords have
been hammered out over a good dinner or a comfortable evening over a glass of wine! More than all the
state meetings at the Foreign Office! Not that the
ladies will get any credit in the history books! Why,
look at Marietta Rockhall! One of the great diplomatic
hostesses of our age! She had the Tsar and that little
Talleyrand man both twisted around her little finger
at the Congress! If it weren't for her *little suppers* in
Vienna, we all might still be in Austria yet! You sister
would do well to take a page from her book." There
was only a whisper of irony in her tone.

"Frankly, Lady Tilghman, I think she feels she's
not up to the job! And I don't think Tilghman has
given her the confidence to go on as she could,"
Sally said flatly.

Comprehension flickered across the old lady's
countenance and she nodded. "*I* could teach her a
thing or two, if she'd but listen to me! I'm not in
my dotage yet!" Her little black eyes sparked and
the ghost of a smile flickered across her thin lips.
"Behind every great man, my dear, there's an even
greater woman who's served her country as she
served her guests! Not to mention her husband. It's
a job that takes two people!"

Sally was very surprised as one of the thin hands
reached out and clutched her own. "I speak frankly

to you, Miss Blythe! But I trust your discretion! You're not taken in a whit by me, are you, my dear?"

"No ma'am, I think not. But my sister is easily intimidated, you see. You terrify her, Lady Tilghman! You must admit you are formidable!"

"And so shall you have to be when you are my age!" Lady Tilghman replied dryly. "Power is all you have left when you become old! But if Julia had but once asked me, I would gladly have helped her!"

"That is between you and my sister," Sally said.

"Diplomacy is too important to be left to the men!" Lady Tilghman exclaimed. "We saw that in the late war. If Julia would but come to me, I think I could help her. I may have withdrawn from the field, but the rules of the game never change!"

She drew up her shoulders and shrugged. "Ah, well! If youth knew, if age could, as they say! You, at any rate, have done far more wisely than anyone expected in choosing William Starret as a husband! You know, Miss Blythe, when you were so particular to Alexander Quartermaine last year, a number of people were holding their breath!"

Sally had no reply for this.

After Lady Tilghman had taken her leave, she realized that the old lady was too proud to offer Julia advice unless she was solicited. And Julia was too intimidated by her grand manner to ask for help. Still and all, she was stung by the old lady's words about Will and Alex, and not a little mortified about the deception.

All of which combined to make her determined to have a confrontation with Julia. Not only was she determined to discover why her sister had tried to pawn those *stupid* rubies, she felt it was also time to reveal her own, equally *stupid* tangle.

Perhaps it was time to cry off!

Unfortunately, when she went upstairs to comfort Julia, a rap on the door brought out Miss Pomfret.

"She's got the headache something terrible, Miss," Pomfret said respectfully but firmly. "She doesn't want to see anyone."

No inducement of Sally's would budge the dresser from the door. Not so much as a glimpse of her sister could Sally get around the dresser's redoubtable form; loyal guardian that she was, Miss Pomfret blocked the door. "She'll come around tomorrow, perhaps."

And with that, Sally had to be satisfied.

But later that evening, when Sally was dressing to attend the Misses Yarrows' rout party alone, Julia, attired in her evening best, slipped out of her room and fled, on silent, silken slippers down the hall and out the door into a coach where a certain dark gentleman waited, a slight, mocking smile on his lips as they drove away.

8

Sally's intention to sit down and have a serious discussion with Julia the next morning, no matter what Miss Pomfret might say or do was detoured by unexpected events.

As a consequence of dancing through a pair of slippers and not coming home until well past midnight under the indulgent chaperonage of Lady Yarrow, it was rather late when Sally arose the next morning. And she only awakened because Betty, very excited, shook her out of a deep and dreamless sleep.

"Oh, Miss, you must get up and get dressed at once! Mr. Starret is downstairs in the street with Mr. Tennant and Mr. Holmes, and they have *hobby horses*!" Betty exclaimed, holding up Sally's robe.

"Hobby horses?" Sally repeated blankly. She rose and allowed Betty to put her into her robe before going to the window and looking down at the street.

She was treated to the sight of Will, Barney, and Frank rolling around the cobbles of Upper Mount Street on the strangest vehicles she had ever seen in her life. They rolled along on narrow wooden frames mounted on two spoked wheels, clutching a handle before them that served as a rudder to allow them to weave in and around the astonished observers. They seemed to be propelling themselves along with their feet, and having a very good time doing it, too.

Will, looking up, caught sight of her hanging out the window and waved his hat in her direction. "Come on down and see the hobby horses!" he cried.

"Oh, Miss, they're the very latest craze," Betty said enviously. "Hobby horses! I saw some boys on them in Green Park last week!"

"I've got to try that!" Sally said, all decorum forgotten. "Will, Will! Wait for me, I'll be right down!"

Will waved again, and just narrowly avoided a collision with a hod cart. The ancient horse drawing it, who probably felt it had seen everything, whinnied and reared, and the teamster turned the crisp morning air blue with his opinion of Will, newfangled contraptions and youth in general.

In a very few minutes, Sally was dressed in a merino pelisse and a bonnet and out on the street. She watched for a while as the gentlemen propelled themselves about, then announced, "I want to try it!"

Will skidded to a stop before her. "You can ride on the crossbar, if you like," he offered handsomely. "You should see how fast I can get this thing goin', Sally! It's amazin'!"

He assisted Sally to mount and waited patiently while she adjusted her full skirts to a more modest coverage, wondering why he'd never noticed what well-turned ankles she had before. "Don't you try to balance, Sal, just sit and let me do that," he said a little gruffly, propelling them along the sidewalk and nearly overturning a footman walking a small dog in the process.

Sally held on to her hat with one hand and the crossbar with the other, Will's arms comfortably keeping her centered as they rolled down the street past a shocked governess, who covered her charge's eyes with her hands.

"Do not look, Jane!" the governess cried as Will and Sally, with Frank and Barney hard behind, rolled around the corner and through the streets of Mayfair.

"Where in the world did you find these?" Sally asked a little breathlessly as they crossed The High and rolled through the iron gates of Hyde Park just in the path of a barouche, whose frightened horses reared in the traces.

"Bought 'em off a fella in Covent Garden, last night. We was comin' from the Cole Hole, and saw him selling them. Well, I guess we were all a trifle foxed, but nothing would do but for Barney to try one out! Well, Frank and I thought, if he can do it, so can we! And so we did! Took us most of the night to figure them out, there's a trick to it, you know, but once we did, we were off and running, so to speak!"

"You are the most complete hand," Sally said admiringly, and Will beamed with pleasure.

"It is something, isn't it?" he asked. "Not everyone could master one of these things, you know!"

"Oh, Will, I want to try it!" Sally pleaded as Frank and then Barney pulled up beside them on the path.

Will looked extremely doubtful. "Don't know if it's the done thing for females," he said slowly.

"Let Sally have a hand," Barney said. "We're all here to make sure she doesn't come to harm. Besides, no one in the park this hour of the morning but us," he explained, thus blithely ignoring several gardeners, a milkmaid, and one or more nursemaids with their infant charges.

"That's our Sally! Pluck to the backbone!" Frank exclaimed. "Come on, gal! Give it a try! We'll spot you!"

Sally wondered if the effects of their night's libations had worn completely away. However, since she was used to their fits and starts, and, as they knew, game for anything. As a child she had climbed as many trees, unstopped as many foxholes, and batted as many cricket balls as anybody, and she was not to be deprived of a chance to try her skill at riding a hobby horse.

In a very short time, not without a great deal of tutoring, Sally was able to maneuver the hobby horse up and down the path without assistance.

It was something entirely different, she thought, to fly along the gravel paths, balancing precariously on the little seat, propelling oneself by pushing one's feet along to get up speed, then lifting one's feet off the ground and balancing over the wheels.

The first time she accomplished this unassisted, the three young men cheered.

"By Jove she's better at it than Miss Quinn!" Frank exclaimed, and received a speaking look from Will for his pains.

For her part, Sally pretended not to notice, but swirled along the gravel, picking up speed as she went, then negotiating a delicate turn and coming back to her companions, flying past them with a roguish toss of her head as she headed in the other direction, ducking her head lest she lose her hat to a low branch growing over the gravel.

Her sister's and her own troubles were quite lost in the moment, and she gave herself over to the pleasure of the company of her old friends, forgetting that she was supposed to be engaged to Will, that she was presumed to be a young lady of fashion as she challenged Frank, then Barney to race with her in and out of the shrubbery as much as if they were all still in the schoolroom.

Still, she would not have been Sally if she had not wondered smugly to herself if the dashing Miss Quinn could master the hobby horse quite as well as she. For the first time, she felt a little stab of jealousy for that pretty actress who had engaged Will's fancy. It surprised her, and she tossed her head, as if the gesture could banish the thought.

Nonetheless, she did not protest when Will demanded his horse back, and she surrendered her seat to him without protest. He placed her back on the seat before him, and she was very aware of his arms nesting around her.

"Penny for your thoughts," he said after a while.

Sally shook her head. "They don't signify at all," she responded. "I wish I might have one of these."

"Not at all the ladylike thing! However, I daresay you could keep one in the country. We could ride down the lanes, you know."

"Would we have to have one for the groom, do you think? Or should I buy one for Betty?" Sally teased.

"Won't need either one of them. Be with your husband," Will replied. He was about to ask her how things were coming with Alex, when he suddenly was conscious of a strong desire not to know.

Hastily, he turned the conversation in a more innocuous direction, and all the way back to Upper Mount Street, they spoke in a desultory fashion about an upcoming balloon ascension to which they had all been invited. Once, when Sally tried to introduce the topic of matters at Tilghman House, Will firmly quelled her. "Not my business and not yours, either, Sally! Told you that earlier! If you start stirring the pot, you will find yourself in the suds, mark my words!"

Sally protested, but Will was adamant.

She only wished she felt more sanguine about Alex's ability to untangle Julia's affairs, whatever they were. But, of course, she reminded herself sternly, Alex must be up to anything!

"You know what?" Sally said finally, "I think someday I would like to see a horrid prize fight, just to see what all of you men enjoy so much!"

Will, very much shocked, replied, "Hobby horses are one thing, Sally . . . prize fights are another matter entirely! Females don't attend them!"

"Not even Miss Quinn?" she quizzed.

"Not even Miss Quinn," he said firmly. "Men only!"

"Sometimes, I think the *world* is for men only," Sally sighed. "It is unfair, you know."

"And I sometimes think the world is spun entirely for females," Will retorted. In a different tone, he muttered, "Oh, bother, there's Alex."

Sally looked up. Sure enough, there *was* Alex, emerging from Tilghman House, drawing on his gloves, his walking stick under one arm. As usual, he was a portrait of the elegant gentleman. There was a sullen look on his face, and when he spotted the caravan of hobby horses coming up the street, his expression did not improve. Rather, he lifted his quizzing glass and stared at them balefully through a hideously magnified eye.

Sally had rather expected he would be amused, that he might say something witty, but instead he merely watched, frigid disapproval emanating from his every pore, as Will assisted Sally to dismount, and Frank and Barney rode in circles around them.

Beneath that cold stare, Sally was suddenly aware that her dress was sadly crumpled, her hair a fright, and her bonnet slightly askew.

"Well, I guess we'll be off," Will said, nodding to

Alex. "I'll see you Wednesday, then, Sally. I'll bring the phaeton and we'll meet the Bingleys there." He signaled to Frank and Barney.

"Yes," she replied abstractly. "Wednesday."

Nodding to Alex, the young men propelled themselves off down the street.

"So, been riding a hobby horse all over Mayfair?" Alex asked in a sullen, disapproving tone as he worked his gloves on, one finger at a time. A muscle in his jaw twitched and his face was dark. "Hardly the sort of behavior one expects from a young lady who wishes to appear tonnish, is it?"

Sally raised her chin defiantly, stung by his criticism, the more because she suspected that it was true; she had behaved very hoydenishly, and had enjoyed herself thoroughly doing it. "I daresay it was shockingly childish of all of us, but it was also a great deal of fun," she said lightly. "Perhaps we'll set a fashion."

She had expected Alex to turn it off with a jest and laugh, but his disapproving mood remained unaltered. "I might expect that sort of collegiate prank from Will and those two, but I held *you* to a higher standard of conduct!" he pronounced.

"If Will has no objection, I fail to see how my conduct should be any of your concern, sir!" she was stung to reply. "Certainly, you of all people have no right to pass judgment upon me, Alex Quartermaine!"

His expression tightened into an impenetrable mask as he reached out and gripped her arm. "You would do well to listen to my advice! Never think because you were born to rank and fortune that I cannot break you to bridle if I chose!"

If it had been anyone else who breathed these words to her, Sally might have been frightened. As it was, she wrenched her arm free of his grasp, a little angry. "Playing it all a little too Gothick, Alex!" she seethed. "I do believe you're jealous!"

The mask dropped from his features as suddenly as it had appeared. It was replaced by his usual mocking smile. "Perhaps I am!" he said lightly, touching his cravat.

His gloves fitted to suit him, he placed his silky high-crowned beaver on his gleaming locks and griped his walking stick. "I hope by this evening you will have quelled that unbecoming independence of yours, for I am engaged to bear you and your sister to the Devonshire House ball. Till then." He tipped his hat and walked off down the street, leaving her staring after him thoughtfully, a faint crease appearing between her brows.

"I want an explanation, Julia!" Sally said without preamble as she burst into her sister's room.

Julia, who had been holding a ball gown in her hands, allowed it to slip through her fingers to the rug, where it lay in a frothy pile at her feet. She had a haggard air, and her embroidered robe looked as if she had been living in it. "Oh, go away, do," she said to Sally. "No, wait, do you have any money lying about?"

Sally looked around the room where gowns and

frocks lay strewn everywhere, like an explosion in a milliner's shop. "Are you running away?" she asked.

"Good God, I wish I could," Julia said, sinking into a chair. She put her hands to her head. "Did Tilghman come home last night or has he moved to his club?"

"I don't know, but I just left Alex on the steps and he was in a rare taking. And the Dowager was here yesterday, trying to find out what's going on between you and Tilghman! I don't think she's as black as you paint her, but that doesn't signify right now! Julia, you've got to tell me what's going on!" Sally demanded. "First there's the Tilghman Rubies—and now this!"

"Oh, I'll be all right! I really will! I'll come about!" Julia said wildly. "I know I will!" She smiled. "I've just drawn the bustle a little, that's all. I've spent a dreadful amount of money on clothes and overdrawn my allowance a little. If Tilghman finds out, he'll kill me! You know what he's like, forever going on about keeping accounts and managing finances. Between my clothes and the remodeling of the house, I've really rowed myself up Tick River." Julia smiled faintly. "At least with Tilghman! I daresay every tradesman in town likes me, however! You don't have a hundred pounds you can let me have till Christmas, do you?"

"I . . . I suppose I do, in my bank accounts, but you know I can't touch Great Aunt Sarah's money without Papa knowing about it. It's tied up in the funds. But I can give you what I have. Julia, what did you do with those rubies? Did you really pawn them?"

Even under duress, Julia was lovely. She simply took on a more haunted beauty. Her eyes grew huge and hollow and luminous, her pale skin seemed to glow. The hands that picked nervously at her dressing gown were thin and graceful. "I didn't think he would notice. I was so *sure* I would get them back before Tilghman found out." Those enormous eyes pinned Sally beneath their gaze. "You wouldn't understand," she said anxiously. "Oh, you are so lucky to have Will! He's so kind and good and commonsensical! Never any Important People to entertain . . ." She picked up a discarded gown that Sally recognized as one she had bought on their shopping expedition. "I don't suppose you'd like to buy this, would you? I'll sell it to you for a quarter of what I owe Celeste . . . "

"Jules, are you selling your clothes, too?" Sally asked.

"You have no idea how much I owe!" Julia cried. "Oh, Sally, I have been such a fool!"

"Well, it can't be so much that you must try to pawn those awful rubies," Sally replied. "Although, I must admit, if I had my choice, they would be the first thing I'd sell, too! I never saw anything so quizzical in my life!"

"I just didn't think he'd find out," Julia said. "It was a very foolish thing to do, I agree. But I was so desperate . . . I kept thinking that something would happen to help me out, but it never does, you know. *Never!*"

"Julia, how much do you owe? Surely you can talk to all these tradesmen, explain to them that you will settle with them next quarter day . . . "

Julia rose and walked across the room. "No, I can't do that. I . . . oh, Sally, you don't understand!"

"No, I don't," Sally admitted. "Julia, I think the best thing you can do is tell Tilghman. He won't beat you, you know! I daresay he would be relieved to know that it's only a few bills!"

"If only it were just a few bills," Julia sighed. "No, I've got to sort these out. Pomfret is going to take them to a second-hand woman she knows of, although she says we'll never get what they're really worth."

"If I might have a word with you alone?" Tilghman knocked on the door and entered at the same time. He did not look pleased, and the look he shot at Sally was hardly one of brotherly affection.

Julia stood up. She looked like Marie Antoinette about to ascend the scaffold.

"I'll talk to you later, Sally," Tilghman said meaningfully.

With no other choice and a sense of increasing foreboding, Sally went to her own boudoir. Perhaps Will was right, and it was not wise to get involved in the Tilghmans' domestic disputes, but would he leave Julia in the lurch, she wondered? The answer was an emphatic no. She went into her own room and picked up a journal, although she could barely focus her attention on it.

It was inevitable that her mind would turn to thoughts of Alex Quartermaine, since such thoughts had sustained her through many a dull hour at Blythe House when her hands were occupied with the pianoforte or needlework or looking after younger brothers and sisters for Miss Pruitt, or any of the other occupations her mother considered suitable for a young lady no longer in the schoolroom. Too old for lessons, confined by the mourning period from attending all but the most sedate neighborhood gatherings, forbidden hunting or any other pleasurable sport for the same reason. Sally had turned inward to a mental landscape in search of relief from boredom. *Idle hands are the devil's workshop* had been a precept of Mrs. Blythe's, but idle minds were a realm outside even that excellent lady's dominion.

Sally had used up many hours of idleness spinning more and more misty and highly romantic fantasies about Alex Quartermaine. And now, confronted with him, in the flesh, so to speak, she was not sure the reality was measuring up to her imagination. The scene on the doorstep this morning was not one she had enjoyed.

Several hours later, her ruminations were interrupted by a knock on the door, and she opened it to find her sister standing there, smiling a small, misty smile.

"Let me in, I can't stand in the hall where the workmen might overhear me," Julia said, slipping into the room and closing the door behind her.

She sank into a lavender bergère chair and sighed, "Well, Tilghman won't be moving to Brook Street, so we are spared that scandal, at least," she said in a thin, drawn voice. "Only imagine what that would have done! I daresay even Mama and Papa would have heard about it, and then they would come down to town."

Her thin hands fluttered over the embroidery on her robe, but she did not meet Julia's eyes. "I told Tilghman that I had been shockingly extravagant, and that I had run up some rather enormous debts. He was very forgiving and said he would take care of the bills and promised to add five hundred pounds to my accounts to hold me till quarter day. And we made up . . ." A little smile played across her face, leaving Sally in no doubt abut how the couple had reconciled their differences. "And he has promised that he will take some time after the end of the Little Season so we can go down to Tilghman Manor, just the two of us, no house guests, no dispatch boxes, no Important People! It will be just like it used to be!" She suddenly looked up at Sally. "Oh, I do love Tilghman, you see! Isn't it ridiculous and unfashionable to be in love with your own husband? And sometimes, I think he loves me just as much as I love him."

For the first time in a long while, she looked really happy. For a moment, Sally believed that all of her sister's many troubles were at an end. But then Julia's hands dropped on the arms of the chair, and her face crumpled. "Oh, Sally, I am the most miserable wretched creature on earth!"

"Are you worried about Lady Rockhall?" Sally asked, kneeling before her sister and taking her hands in her own.

"Oh, that, too!" Julia sighed bitterly. Her fingers tightened around her sister's hands. "But I didn't tell Tilghman *everything*, you see! I should have, I know I should have, but I could not bring myself to do so! I . . . I was so happy that we seemed to have reached an accord after so much misunderstanding! I know it was foolish of me, but after tonight, I know that everything will be all right, I just know it! My luck is changing, you see! And I have five hundred pounds!"

"Julia, what are you talking about?" Sally demanded. "You make no sense at all!"

"I'm sure I can win it all back, you see! We go to Devonshire House tonight, and you know that the Duchess always has the most amazingly high stakes in faro. I am sure to win enough to pay off my vowels!"

"Your . . . vowels?" Sally asked, all at sea.

"My I.O.U.s, of course!" Julia beamed. "I am quite in the basket, you see. But I will come about now, I know that I will."

"Gambling? You've been gambling?" Sally demanded. "Oh, Julia! What a stupid thing to do! You have never had the least head for cards!"

Julia looked hurt. "How can you say so? I always swept the board at silver-loo?"

"Julia, how much do you owe?"

Her sister shrugged. "Not so very much! I mean, it's the merest trifle, really! Besides, I know I shall come about! Alex says it is always so, that just when one thinks one's luck has run out, and it is all low tide, one's luck changes immediately! And just look! This morning, I thought I was quite adrift, but now I have five hundred pounds with which to play!"

"How much do you owe, Jules?" Sally repeated.

Julia looked defiantly at her. "Not so very much! Only five thousand pounds!"

Sally sat down, hard, on the floor at her sister's feet. Heiress she might be to an unexpected legacy, but five thousand pounds was more than she had ever dreamed of seeing in one place at one time. "Oh, dear," was all she could think of to say.

"You mustn't tell Tilghman!" Julia said quickly. "He would be so angry, and just when everything is going so well again. You know how much he dislikes gaming. He considers it frivolous! But, really, it's quite fashionable, and *everyone* does it! Why, Lord Petersham thinks nothing of sitting down to the table and playing for fifty guinea points."

"Perhaps, but you are not Lord Petersham, and what's more, if you've been playing cards with the Carlton House set, you're much more depraved than I thought! They're all shockingly decadent for one thing and, worse, they're all quite *middle-aged* for another."

"Oh, what kind of a flat do you take me for?" Julia cried, quite offended. "As if I would do anything as unfashionable as run with the Prince Regent and his set! No, I thank you."

"But, still, you must have been *somewhere* to gamble away five thousand pounds. Oh, Julia, how could you?"

"You needn't look at me like that! Why, all the most tonnish people play cards! You can't say that *Alex* is not all the crack! And he plays pretty heavily, let me tell you! And any number of other really fashionable people!"

As Julia said, gambling for high stakes was a part of fashionable life. All the gentlemen's clubs on Brook Street offered play, and even Almack's had its card tables. No hostess worth her reputation would dream of presenting an entertainment that did not feature card tables, and Will himself had often boasted his winnings or mourned his losses at horse races and boxing matches. The stories of a person's entire fortune doubling or being lost on the turn of card were a standard part of London gossip.

But, gambling was rarely a part of a debutante's life. Young, unmarried females might play a hand or two of whist or piquet or silver-loo, but rarely did they enter into serious play when there was dancing and parties to occupy their time. Still, Sally reflected, the Marriage Mart played for the highest stakes of all—a young person's entire future. Although Sally had been dimly aware that Alex played, she had no idea that he played heavily. A dreadful suspicion entered her mind, and she flicked it away.

"So you sold the Tilghman Rubies to pay your gaming debts?" she asked Julia aloud.

"Not sold, *pawned!* I thought I could get the money back and replaced the rubies before Tilghman noticed, but it didn't work out that way," Julia sighed bitterly.

"So it wasn't for dressmaker's bills."

"Not entirely! And you know that one must pay one's gaming debtors whatever else one ignores!"

"Oh, lord, what a tangle! It makes my poor scheme look like nothing," Sally muttered.

"What?"

This, Sally decided, was not the time to enlighten her sister about the Banbury tale she and Will had worked out concerning their "engagement." There were more pressing matters at hand.

"Julia, why do you think that you will recover yourself tonight? Will says that when one particularly needs to win, that is inevitably when one loses!"

"Will's a slow-top and knows nothing of it," Julia replied with some asperity.

"As if you did!" Sally retorted. "But how did you ever enter into such a shocking amount of debt? I didn't have the faintest idea!"

Julia leaned back in the bergère chair and closed her eyes. "It just happened. I mean, Tilghman works all the time, and never accompanies me when I go out, and Alex suddenly reappeared in town, and he knew of all these really amusing places and people, he took me to Devonshire House, and you can't imagine how exciting it was, at first, to win. And, of course, with Alex to teach me, I was winning and winning all the time!"

"Beginner's luck!" Sally suggested.

"Perhaps. But then, Alex took me to this house on Half Moon Street, the most amusing people, you can't imagine. Mrs. Bedford, it's her house, you

see, has these exclusive little card parties. Well, I
thought she was very tonnish at first, after all,
everyone went there, the most fashionable people
like Georgianna Devonshire, Lady Bedlington, Sir
Waldo Frant, Lady Sarah Repton—it was all the
crack, I thought! You can't conceive how exciting it
was, at first, to play. Of course, I was still playing
for chicken stakes, but when I saw how easy it was
to win, I started to up the stakes. And then I started
to lose! So, of course, I had to play some more,
thinking, you know, to cover my losses, but I kept
losing and the stakes kept going up and up and—
well, there you have it! The next thing I knew, I
owed Mrs. Bedford and Alex and everyone! It all
happened so fast!" Julia blinked.

"Georgianna Devonshire, Marian Bedlington,
Sir Waldo Frant, Lady Sarah Repton—" Sally
repeated. "Gamesters all of them! Even I know
that. Oh, Julia, how could Alex let you dip so
deep?"

"I owe *him* quite a bit of money, too," Julia
sighed.

"Oh, Julia," Sally shook her head. "You did not
play against him, too?"

"Well, it was not precisely play," Julia admitted.
"I bet him a thousand pounds that one raindrop
would travel faster down the windowpane than
another. It was foolish, but . . . well, there you have
it. I was so bored before. And now I wish I were
bored again!" She placed her face in her hands.
"And it seems as if the house will never be remod-
eled, and if Tilghman finds out about this, every-

thing will be all over! He'll surely end up in Lady Rockhall's arms then!"

"Please don't make a watering pot of yourself," Sally commanded. "I'm sure there must be a way out of this. I just don't know what it is!"

"Well, I do! I'll wager Tilghman's five hundred and I'll win it all back!" Julia declared.

9

Devonshire House was one of the grandest mansions in Mayfair. The old duke, who had lived in such a scandalous ménage à trois with his high-rolling duchess and their great and good friend Lady Elizabeth Foster, had died, and the new duke, a much different man, was said to be very much in love with the Princess of Wales, and she with him. There was much speculation around that time that one of the richest men in England might make a match of it with the heiress to the throne. Accordingly, the dowager duchess was doing everything there was in her power to accomplish the match, including a series of very gay balls and parties at which Princess Charlotte was always guest of honor.

If she had not been so distracted with Julia's problems, Sally would have very much enjoyed being a part of the company at the ball given that evening, for she was only a year or two younger than the lady who would someday be her sovereign, and was curious to meet the future queen.

Alex, in his corbeau-colored evening dress had called for Julie and Sally a half-hour before the event, and the sisters, in their finest, had been ready, for they knew that it would be at least an hour's wait in the lumbering coach line before their vehicle reached its turn at the canopied entrance to Devonshire House, so long did it take for each carriage to discharge its passengers.

Julia was highly nervous in anticipation; the plumes in her headdress bobbed and wove as she chattered on anxiously about the evening ahead and the card tables awaiting her attention. Her gloved hands played with her reticule and she fingered her diamonds nervously.

"Do you really think Julia can come about one evening?" Sally baldly demanded of Alex in the darkness of the coach.

He looked at her from beneath his lashes eyes and smiled. "Ah, so the schoolroom miss has learned some of our secrets!"

"Well, she is my sister, Alex and as such, I had to tell her something!" Julia replied, with skittish laugh. She tapped Alex's arm with her fan. "After all, she may yet have to bail me out of the suds, being our little heiress!"

"Heiress?" Alex repeated casually. He looked through the dim light at Sally.

"Oh, yes, Sally has quite fifty thousand pounds at her disposal now," Julia announced carelessly. She leaned forward and craned her neck out the window. "Oh, we're still miles away from the door. That's the trouble with going to parties in one's own neighborhood, you know, one never knows whether one should walk or take the coach! Everyone complains about it, but in the end everyone always summons the coachman!"

"Fifty thousand pounds! Sally, how came you not to tell your old friends this great piece of news?" Alex asked, touching his perfectly tied cravat with two fingers.

Sally flushed, uncomfortable with the subject and annoyed with Julia for her artless, nervous prattle. One's fortune, like the most intimate details of the marital bed, was something people simply did not bandy about casually.

"Perhaps I didn't think it was important," she said tersely. "Certainly, Will never considered it so!" She wondered where this last piece of information had come from; certainly it had not sprung, a full-fledged thought, from her mind!

"Oh, I am sure Will took it into consideration," Alex said lightly. "Only think how many hobby horses one could buy with such a fortune!"

Sally opened and closed her mouth. It had been on the tip of her tongue to apologize again for that episode, but why should she owe Alex amends when she had done nothing wrong?

As if sensing that he had stepped, if only for a moment, on thin ice, Alex asserted himself to be agreeable. "I hope you will allow me to waltz with you this evening! And I will be certain to make sure that you meet the princess! It will be something to tell your grandchildren about, you know."

"If you can tear yourself away from the card tables," Sally replied a little coolly. "I think it is Julia who will need all of your attention tonight."

Alex made a little tsking sound, but leaned back in the carriage seat, regarding her with a maddening little smile, clearly amused. "You're so pretty when you're irritated, you know! Your eyes sparkle, your cheeks flame! Most attractive!"

Perhaps fortunately, at point, one of the footmen opened the door to allow the ladies to descend, and Sally was not forced to make a reply.

They waited for several minutes in an icy anteroom with many other arriving guests while their cards were given to Devonshire House footmen who in turn, passed them on to the majordomo, who stood at the top of the stairs and announced them in a resonate voice to those already assembled in the ballroom on the third floor. As they were handed up the steps through the forest of liveried pages Devonshire House considered appropriate to the occasion, Sally privately wondered if Princess Charlotte, who had been brought up in modest sequestration at Windsor Castle and Warwick House, would find Devonshire House too grand for even a royal heiress.

"This makes Tilghman House look like a cottage, doesn't it?" Julia mischievously whispered in her sister's ear as they surmounted the last grand staircase and were announced into the presence of the Duke and Dowager Duchess, who received them very grandly indeed before passing them into the company. The ballroom, Julia noted, was draped in pink silk . . . so very ordinary!

Here, all the ladies were anxious to claim Alex's attention, and he was soon occupied with a great deal of bowing and hand kissing. Other members of Julia's court took up the gap by surrounding her and Sally and diverting them with generous compliments and the latest on-dits of many of the august personages assembled. The bachelor Duke was considered the highest prize on the Marriage Mart, and it was vastly amusing for those in the know to watch the hopeful mamas swim through the room with their eligible daughters in tow, hoping to attract the notice of His Grace.

After a while, there was a little hush, and then in a very resonant voice indeed, Her Royal Highness, the Princess Charlotte, Princess of Wales was announced, together with her entourage, and a tall blonde girl in peach satin and a diamond parure came down the stairs in a mannish stride, acknowledging the bows and curtseys to the left and to the right. Sally, who had wanted her to look a little more fairy-like and a little less Hanoverian, was a little disappointed, but Julia pronounced Her Royal Highness as being much in looks this evening.

The Princess opened the ball by dancing the quadrille with the ancient Duke of Bergamot, and soon afterwards, Sally found herself claimed by the Honorable Barney Tennant, who scribbled something on her dance card, took her into his arms, and breathed, "Help me, Sally! Marriage-minded mamas everywhere!" in tones of deep panic as he spun her out on the dance floor.

From there well on, Sally never sat down, as her hand was claimed time after time for the first series of dances. She lost sight entirely of Julia, and assumed that her sister had made her way directly to the card room. Certainly there were no nodding plume headdresses to be seen in the crush of dancers on the floor.

She did however, pass Lady Rockhall once as she was whirled about the floor in the reel by an earnest young viscount. Her ladyship was in the arms of a very dashing gentleman with an eye patch and a great many decorations, and Sally could have sworn that illustrious lady actually *winked* at her as she glided majestically past, breathtakingly fashionable in *eau-de-Nil* crêpe and some quite resplendent emeralds.

But it could not have been; august females like Lady Rockhall never winked at insignificant little chits like Sally. Or did they? In spite of Julia, she liked Lady Rockhall, and thought that when she was that age, there was nothing she would like more than to be just like her; independent, fashionable, powerful, and beautiful.

"Penny for your thoughts," a voice said and Sally found herself looking up into Will's smiling face.

"Oh," she exclaimed involuntarily. "How very glad I am to see you! I never thought you would come here, as much as you dislike these sad squeezes!"

"If it's not a squeeze, it's not a success," he grinned, placing a hand on her waist and setting off to the strains of the waltz. He was at his most handsome, in somber black evening clothes and a cravat tied in the style known as the *trone d' amour*. She doubted any gentleman in the room could look as fine as Will, when he was turned out in knee britches and silk stockings that showed off his well-shaped legs, and said so.

Will flushed with pleasure. "I could say the same of you. That's a very fetching dress!"

Since she was wearing celestial blue lutestring trimmed with corded point and a great deal of French work, and knew she looked very nice, she received this compliment with a smile.

"Oh, Will! I think I promised this dance to Harry Gordon!" she recalled after a minute.

"I asked him if he minded; said a man had a right to dance with his own fiancée, don't you know! Harry had no problem with that. I'll take you down to supper, too."

"Yes," Sally said a little wistfully, "I suppose a man does have a right to dance with his own fiancée."

"Don't know why it should be, but I had a great fancy to come at the last minute," Will said. "So I threw on my togs and came around."

"I am very glad you did!" Sally said, putting her head against his shoulder for a second. "Now we can be comfortable!"

"Yes, comfortable," Will said, looking down at the glistening copper head on his shoulder with an odd, longing look on his face. Unaware of his expression, Sally closed her eyes for a moment and inhaled the essential scent of Will; clean shirts and maleness and a faint whisper of soap. She found it oddly pleasant.

"I see you are wearing your pearls," Will remarked. He touched them where they rested against the nape of her neck. "They are very becoming on you."

"Thank you," Sally said, bringing herself back into the present.

The waltz ended and they applauded politely. Her Royal Highness having departed, the company became a little more relaxed. But not much; Devonshire House was much too grand for anyone to feel totally relaxed in its vast, formal rooms. Will gave Sally his arm and they went down to the supper room.

It was not until Julia had consumed several lobster patties and a number of helpings of green peas that she recalled her sister with a small guilty jolt.

"Oh, Will! We've got to look in on Julia in the card room! No doubt if she is losing, she will be very glad of someone to take her down to supper!"

In the card room, several tables had been set up and were in active use. Sally blinked at the great number and variety of gamesters at the tables, women and men alike, of all ages and conditions involved in what even she could see was very serious play. Great piles of golden guineas, as well as small scribbled slips of paper bearing the vowels of the losers were scattered across each of the green baize-covered tables. Footmen circulated among the guests refilling glasses and proffering trays of food, which sat by the elbows of the players on small occasional tables. It was the sole duty of one servant to provide fresh packs of cards and dice at the beginning of each round of play. The world outside might not have existed for these players; their faces betrayed nothing but an intense concentration for the game at hand, without so much as a few words of conversation.

Sally spied Julia and Alex at one table, hard at faro with a choleric-looking older man and a glint-eyed female of uncertain years but, to judge by the amount of her stake, certain fortune. Julia's plumes were looking very limp indeed, and there was a very small pile of counters before her.

"Doesn't look too good," Will said to Sally in an undertone. "And what a pair to play with! Lord Hamilton and Mrs. Sayre! Deep bettors, both of them."

Sally shivered, following Alex across the room toward her sister's table.

Sally watched as Alex took the faro box and shot two cards toward the older man, who smiled grimly and discarded cards on the painted baize, where diagrams laid out the faces of the pasteboards.

"Done!" Julia said with a high laugh, tossing her hand on the table. "Will you take another vowel, Hamilton?"

The older man nodded curtly, anxious to open another hand.

"We came to see if we could take you down to supper, Julia," Will said. "Thought you might be glad of a break."

"Hold on now, we're playing!" said the older woman, clutching the faro box to her spare chest.

Julia looked relieved. "Yes, I think I could do with a break," she said in a tight little voice. "Perhaps it will change my luck, which has been abominable all night!"

Sally sighed. Alex, looking up at Will, smiled. "Perhaps you'd like to sit in?"

Will shook his head. "No, I thank you! Faro ain't my game! Looks like it ain't Julia's either!"

Alex shrugged, indifferently. "Perhaps not! But I hate to leave the table when the luck's running my way!"

"Are you in or out, Lady Tilghman?" Mrs. Sayre asked impatiently.

"Perhaps just one more hand," Julia said, but Will tapped her on the shoulder.

"Should be very glad if you would allow me to escort you to the supper room," he said.

Alex shot him a look, then with a show of difference, turned back to play.

Julia rose from the table and allowed Will to lead her out of the room, Sally following them closely.

"How much are you down?" she demanded of her sister as they made their way down the steps from the ballroom to the supper room.

"For God's sake, Sally, *smile!*" Julia commanded in a hiss as she nodded to several acquaintances on the stairs. "Only four hundred and thirty pounds! I still have seventy to play with."

"That's just grand," Sally replied, smiling with

all her teeth. "Julia, how did you *ever* become such a blockhead?"

"Much you know about it!" Julia retorted. Her plumes quivered with indignation.

"Well, I know enough not to do it!"

Will, who had been listening to all of this, frowned. "Badly dipped, Jules?" he asked sympathetically.

"Worse than you know!" Sally said, unable to hold her tongue.

As they went into the supper room, where a handsome buffet was being served from a long table by yet more footmen, Julia took on a sullen look, allowing Will to make her up a plate without much caring what he caused to be piled upon it.

"I don't care what you say to Will, but I wish you would not bring my affairs into it! I'm a married woman and I'm *perfectly* capable of handling my own business!" Julia announced to her sister as they took a seat at one of the little tables scattered around the room. "You may as well drag Robby into it!"

"Well, I think you ought to talk to Will about it, at least! Believe me, he is a complete hand. He *always* knows what to do when one is in the suds!"

"Really, Sally! I . . ." Julia started to say, then Will came and sat down, presenting each lady with a plate heaped with lobster patties and other temptations. Julia looked down at her food without interest. A footman came past them, pouring wine into their glasses, and she drained hers in one motion.

"Oh, no! Not my business!" Will said in response to a pleading look from Sally. "Told your sister, Jules, if there's a problem, Tilghman's the one you ought to apply to!"

"Tilghman's a part of the problem," Julia sighed gloomily. "Besides, there's nothing anyone can do for me. I ought to just pack up my things and move home to Mama and Papa."

"That bad?" Will asked, much against his own better judgment.

"You don't know the half of it!" Julia twisted the damask napkin through her fingers. "If Alex can't help me, how can you?"

"I ain't Alex. Never pretended to be! What's more, wouldn't want to be him if I could!" Will protested. "All very well, of course, but there you have it. Anyway," he added with true nobility, "if an old friend can't offer you a hand, who can?"

Julia looked at him hard.

"Will can help you, I know it," Sally said.

"As long as it don't involve man-woman things. Sally can tell you I'm not very good at that line."

"That's not true at all!" Sally protested. "Julia, tell him!"

So Julia did. In fits and starts, with many promptings and proddings from Sally, the whole story came tumbling out for examination.

"Five thousand pounds!" Will exclaimed at one point of disclosure, and he had to be shushed by both sisters lest others in the supper room overhear them.

Three heads, one with nodding plumes, bent together.

"Well, you are in the basket," Will said when Julia had finished. "And I still think the best thing to do would be to make a clean breast of all of it to Tilghman. Five thousand pounds ain't likely to damage him; daresay since he's as rich as a nabob, he'll think it a trifle and tell you not to gamble any more, which is what I think you should do. Lay off the pasteboards."

"Well, there's always E. O."

"No, no dice either!" Will said firmly. "No horses, no crackbrained wagers, nothing! Find another interest! Tell you one thing, Jules. When you're badly dipped, your luck don't change! Take it from me, I know! There was this time when I was down at Oxford . . . but that's a dead bore."

Will called for more wine, and while the two sisters watched him hopefully, he thought long and hard.

"What I don't understand," he said at last, "is why Alex didn't stop you before you dipped any deeper! Not a right thing to do!"

"Don't blame Alex for this, Will! You know he would never drag Julia into anything! She's quite capable of doing it all herself!" Sally said loyally.

Will threw her a look. "Lord knows, he's gamed enough to know when to turn a flat away!" he said, shaking his head.

"I am not a flat!" Julia protested. "Why, even Mrs. Bedford said that I was a an out-and-outer!"

Will's eyebrows rose. "Mrs. Bedford, did you say?" he asked. "How did you fall in with old Mother Bedford?"

"She's quite respectable! Her card parties are all the crack!" Julia said. "And she's been very good about waiting for the money I owe her—"

"Don't tell me you owe her that five thousand pounds," Will said darkly. "Good God, the Bedford woman runs one of the most infamous hells in town! Everyone knows that but you, Julia! It was very bad of Alex to take you there! He's steered you there, I'll wager, and collects a commission on all that you lose!"

"No, he cannot!" Sally interjected. "Not Alex!"

But Julia, wide-eyed, nodded. "That was why I had to pawn the Tilghman Rubies!"

"What?" Will leaned closer to her, as if he could not quite believe the turn this was all taking. "Rubies, did you say? Jules, you didn't ask Alex to pawn your rubies for you?"

"Well, yes, but I didn't think that was important," Julia said.

"You sent Alex to pawn them?" Sally asked. "And he did it?"

Julia nodded. "He was glad to oblige me!"

"And was it his idea?" Will asked. "Did he tell you if you needed the cash to pay Mrs. Bedford, pawning the Tilghman Rubies was the thing to do?"

"Well, I never would have thought of it, and I thought it was an extremely clever idea, because I never wear them, and so Tilghman wouldn't miss them before I'd won enough money back to come and get them again."

"And, I suppose, Alex collected a commission on

the sale, too! Of course he would! Since he was the one who introduced you to Mrs. Bedford, and encouraged you to play deep at her house? Oh, Julia, you *are* a flat!" Will shook his head. "Thank God Mr. Hamlet brought them back. Except now you still owe five thousand pounds."

Sally clutched his arm. "Will, where is all this leading?" she asked.

He threw her a long blue-eyed look. "Nowhere you want to go," he replied, putting his hand over hers. "I'm sorry, Sally."

"I don't understand," Julia said, looking from one of them to the other. "What are you trying to say, Will?"

He frowned. "I'm not entirely sure where I'm going with all of this, but I can tell you this; I don't much like it!"

"Al . . . Alex has done something very wrong. That's what you think, isn't it, Will?" Sally asked with a sinking heart.

"That's what I suspect," Will said quietly.

Sally straightened. "I can't believe it! I don't want to believe it! Why would Alex want to hurt Julia?"

"It's not a question of hurting Jules, it's getting what he wants," Will conjectured. "I suppose if one cared to look, one would find that Alexander Quartermaine doesn't have a feather to fly with!"

"Not Alex," Julia said in a shaking voice. "Oh, not Alex! He has been such a friend to me, always there, never any sort of impropriety, the sort one finds with some of one's male friends—" she broke off, shaking her head. "Oh, I can't believe it!"

"I don't understand! What are you saying about Alex?" Sally demanded, deeply puzzled. "Julia, Alex is your friend! You can't possibly believe that he would do anything to hurt you! Or me, either! He would never want to hurt me! Oh, Will, I think you're just jealous! You know that you and Barney and Frank never did like Alex! And Tilghman doesn't like him either, you can tell!"

"Sally, please! Keep your voice down! People are staring at you! Will, I have developed a headache, and I would like to go home, if we can have your escort," Julia said.

"I would agree with you," Will said, rising from the table. "Sally, can we carry on this discussion in private?"

Sally's mind was spinning. She was finding it very hard to accept the direction in which Will's conjectures were taking them.

"I can't believe you are listening to all of this," she said to Julia.

"And I cannot believe you are not," Julia retorted. "Particularly when you are forever telling me that Will is always right and advising me to place my confidence in his counsel!"

"Ah, here you all are! Sally, I hope you recall you have promised the next waltz to me!"

Sally turned to see Alex standing behind her, smiling his lazy smile down upon her like a shower of liquid silver. He offered her his hands.

"Yes," she said in a shaking voice. "I have remembered! Unfortunately, Julia has developed a headache and needs to go home! Will has been

so very kind as to offer his escort to her, so perhaps you will be kind enough to offer me yours,
Alex!"

With shaking hands, she withdrew the emerald
from her hand and handed it to Will. "I don't think
I will need this anymore, thank you!" she said
coldly.

"Sally!" Julia cried.

Will, his expression impassive, accepted the ring
and gave her a short bow. "Just as you wish!" he
said. He offered Julia his arm. "Ready to leave?" he
asked her.

Julia rose. "More than ready! Sally, I shall expect
you home directly!"

Plumes nodding majestically, she swept out of
the supper room on Will's arm.

Sally flushed to the roots of her hair, deeply and
acutely aware that everyone in the room was staring at her and that the story that she had handed
Will his ring back would ripple through Devonshire House and out into the Polite World before
the evening was over.

Alex was laughing softly. "Well done, little one! I
didn't know you had such a sense of drama in you!
Should I offer you my sympathies?"

"You may offer me your congratulations! I have
just discovered that . . . that Mr. Starret and I
should not suit at all! Our opinions are too far
divided on a number of important subjects!"

"Ah," Mr. Quartermaine said, offering Sally his
arm. "Shall we dance?"

"Yes!" Sally said, and mustering what dignity

she could, removed herself from the room under his escort.

When they were out on the floor, and she was in his arms, looking up into his handsome face, she sighed.

"Is it too much to hope that I shall see more of you now?" Alex asked her, his dark eyes serious.

"No, I should like that very much," she replied.

"So would I," he said. "My hopes have been raised a great deal by this evening. You and Starret would never suit anyway!"

"Oh, why not?"

Alex shrugged one well-tailored shoulder. "Because he might know what you need, but I know what you want," he said in a low voice, holding her just a little more tightly in his grip.

A small frisk passed through Sally's body, and she sighed.

"May one ask what you and Will argued about?" Alex inquired, his lips very close to her ear.

"You, actually," Sally said before she could stop herself. She was angry, and she knew that when she was angry, her common sense frequently deserted her. But still, when she was with Alex, it was as if she were wax in his hands.

"Ah! And what, may I ask, makes me a subject fit for argument?" he asked lightly.

"Will thinks you are not quite good enough for me," she said.

Alex stiffened; she felt this, and sensed immediately that she had gone too far. If she came out and repeated Will's accusations, then Alex might challenge Will to a duel. Certainly, he would have every right to do so. Will had leveled, indirectly, some very serious charges against Alex. He had accused him of things no gentleman would ever do! Not, of course, that she, Sally believed it all for one minute, but the idea that Alex might challenge Will to a duel because of her runaway tongue was enough to frighten her. Not only would it be a dreadful scandal, but what if Alex hurt or worse, killed Will? Everyone knew that Alex was a crack swordsman. And as angry as she was with Will, she certainly didn't wish him to be hurt on her account.

"We just don't suit, Will and I," she said quickly. "It's really of no consequence."

"It is to me! I have a feeling, little one, that you are not telling me all!"

"There's nothing else to tell! Really!" Sally repeated brightly.

Alex looked down at her, his lips set into a thin line, a hard little glint in his dark eyes that somehow frightened her a little. She had seen that same look on his face that morning and had not liked it then.

But as quickly as it had come, it was gone, and he was all smiles and compliments again, turning the conversation to inconsequentials with so much polished charm that she quite thought she had escaped.

A little while later, when his phaeton pulled up before the door at Upper Mount Street, he pressed her fingers against his lips. "Now, I hope I shall see a great deal more of you," he said. "This time I don't mean to allow you to escape me, little one."

Sally wondered why she did not feel as if her plan had finally come to fruition.

10

"Good morning, Miss. My lady would like to see you in her room as soon as convenient," Betty said as she drew back the curtains up on a rainy September morning.

The first words Sally heard when she awakened did little to improve her mood. She had not spent a restful night. Nonetheless, she dutifully padded down the long hallway to Julia's room as soon as Betty had completed her morning toilette.

She found Julia still in bed, with a tray across her knees and Pomfret clucking her tongue as she picked up her discarding clothing from the night before.

"That will be all for now, Pomfret. I'll ring when I need you," Julia said, eyeing her sister with something very much like dislike.

No sooner had the abigail closed the door behind her than Julia was out of bed, flinging her robe on. "Sally, how *could* you?" Julia asked. "Alex is such a viper!"

"He is *not!*" Sally retorted. "You know perfectly well that you got yourself into this tangle. Alex didn't hold a pistol to your head!"

"Well, he seems to have made a handsome profit from me," Julia replied. "And I trusted him because he was your friend."

"He's still my friend!" Sally cried hotly. "How can you listen to Will? He's . . . he's just *jealous* because he's not as handsome nor as tonnish as Alex!"

"Why did you give Will back his ring? You're a fool, Sally, if you think there's a better man than Will Starret—" Julia broke off. "Oh, I began to see it all now! You think Alex will come up to scratch! Well, I am sure he will, now that I've blurted out the fact that you have fifty thousand pounds! Unless, of course he can find another heiress with an even greater fortune!"

"What on earth do you mean?" Sally asked. "Alex liked me when I did not have fifty thousand pounds!"

Julia shook her head. "Oh, Sally, how *could* you not know? Everyone does! Oh, Mama should have told you! Alex doesn't have a feather to fly with! But of course, Mama was so sure that you and Will would make a match of it that it never occurred to her that you might be interested in Alex! How very like Mama that is! And," she added naively, "people think *I* have no common sense! Oh, Sally! Alex must marry a female with a fortune!"

"I don't believe it!" Sally cried. "He was so attentive to me last Season when I had no fortune!"

"Oh, Sally, you were one of Alex's flirts! Didn't you know that? Oh, why didn't Mama tell you these things! It is because she lives in the country and doesn't know the ways of the world, I suppose. That flirting, making you feel as if you're the only woman in the world is what makes Alex so particularly charming, you know! And that is fatal! Sally, don't tell me you threw Will over because of Alex?" Julia was truly horrified. "And in front of everyone, too! Oh, Sally!"

Sally sank into a chair. "You're just telling me these things because you believe Will," she said. But reality, as ugly as it was at that moment, was almost beginning to sink in. "But I love him!" she cried, as if that emotion could somehow carry the day in her favor.

"Well, perhaps you think you do," Julia conceded with some sympathy. "If I didn't love Tilghman so much, I could see where one could be madly infatuated with Alex. He really is handsome, you know. But when I think about how he has taken me in with Mrs. Bedford and the rubies, I am quite inclined to scratch his eyes out! There's only one thing for it, Sally! You must send Will a note immediately and tell him you are very sorry, but he was right and you were wrong!"

"No, I can't do that," Sally said in a soft voice. "Oh, Julia, I have been such a fool, and now there's no way out." The whole story of her deception with Will came pouring out.

Julia listened with astonishment. Every now and then she made a little noise, and once, she clasped her hands together and raised her eyes heavenward. But, on the whole, she took it rather better than Sally had expected. Perhaps, being Sally's sister, Julia was beyond surprise at anything her sibling might do. "Poor Mama and Papa and the Starrets, too!" she said after Sally had finished. "And poor you, too! Oh, Sally, how could you do such a thing? How could Will? And not tell me! Oh, dear, what a scandal this would cause if anyone knew about it! Well, there's only one thing to do, and that's to pretend it never happened at all! Thank God there were no announcements sent to the papers! And it's the end of the Season, so perhaps no one will notice. But all for Alex? Sally, you must be mad! I suppose we shall have to tell Tilghman, but he will take it well enough. Which is more than I can say will happen when I tell him that I've been led to a gambling hell, which is what Mrs. Bedford's is, Will says, and fleeced of five thousand pounds! Then I suppose I shall have to go back to Blythe House!" She looked very downcast as she said this.

"Oh, I am so tired of you and your five thousand pounds!" Sally said suddenly. "You know that you shall have to tell Tilghman the whole of it, and he'll be angry for about three seconds, then he'll pay it, and you'll just go on and get yourself into another scrape as soon as you get bored!"

Julia blinked. "You're talking to *me* about a scrape? Are you expecting your courses, Sally?" she asked. "You are always a little out of sorts around that time of the month, you know! Here, write Will a note and you will feel better."

"It won't do any good!" Sally said. "He will not come around!" She stormed out of the room and went into her own room, where she sat sulking.

When word came upstairs that Mr. Quartermaine was here, hoping she might like to ride, she changed quickly into her habit and left the house.

"I was afraid of this," Will said, standing with his back to the fire. "But I am glad that she made a clean breast of it to you. I must have been mad to go along."

"She didn't even want to listen to me," Julia said. "I had no idea that her feelings were so strong for Alex."

"I had some idea," Will said lightly. "I never really liked Alex," he added in a matter-of-fact tone. "But knowing what I know now, I cannot say that I am surprised."

"I wish I were more so! But Alex is such good ton, you know, and he goes everywhere! I've never been so taken in my life! How was I to know Mrs. Bedford was running a hell?"

"You weren't. But damme, Julia, didn't you have the idea that the cards might be fuzzed or the dice loaded?"

"None whatsoever! I was sadly taken in. I thought Mrs. Bedford a most respectable woman! I *am* a flat! And the worst of it is that I thought Alex was my friend, not a greeking Captain Sharp!" She wrung her hands together. "Will, she refused to listen to me! I don't know what to do short of forbidding her to leave her room, and you can imagine how well she'd listen to me on that score! Good God, can you imagine the scandal-broth we've brewed? I wasn't proud of her last night at all, and now she's out riding with Alex! Thank God, no one goes into the park this early in the morning!"

"Yes, I suppose so. But when Sally makes her mind up, there's nothing that can change it," Will said thoughtfully.

"But to cry off from your engagement! And in such a public way! Mama and Papa would have been horrified!"

"Well, I daresay it wouldn't have worked out anyway," Will replied. "I suppose Alex is who she wanted all along."

"You're being so stoic, Will!" Julia said with a great deal of feeling. "I know this must be difficult for you."

Will was silent for a long period of time, his back still turned toward Julia so that she could not read his expression.

Lady Tilghman, who had always placed great faith in the superior wisdom of almost any character stronger than her own, watched him hopefully.

"I would like," Will said at last, squaring his shoulders, "to wring her neck! But that would not do, I think. I've danced to Sally's tune a great deal too long for her good, and certainly for my own. It's time she had a taste of her own treatment, as my old Nanny used to say. As impossible as her conduct has been of late, I still don't like to see her thrown! She might catch cold! Julia, I want you to listen to me very carefully, and do exactly as I ask you, and we all may come out of this on top of the blanket!"

Julia leaned forward.

As he sat looking out the bow window of Brooks Club into St. James's Street, watching the traffic, Alex Quartermaine seemed the picture of a gentleman of fashion without a care in the world. Sipping from a glass of wine, he was lounging carelessly in his club chair, his eyes hooded, a faint smile playing on his lips. Impeccably attired in a bottle coat of Bath superfine and a pair of biscuit-hued pantaloons, his elegant cravat tied in the Obaldstone, he was, to any interested viewer, the epitome of a gentleman who could proclaim the world his oyster. No one would have thought that his mind was spinning, weaving, desperately seeking a plan to deliver him from his troubles.

That morning, the bailiffs had been in his rooms.

It had been a trifling sum demanded by his harness-maker on a bill nearly twelve months due, but it had been enough to frighten him into considering his future. No one who looked at him would be dreamed that he was considering desperate measures.

Alexander Quartermaine was spoiled. Handsome, well-birthed, he was the posthumous and only child of a mother who had brought him up to believe that his every action was perfection, who no more would have dreamed of checking his

behavior than disinheriting him from what small
fortune she possessed. It had been her ambition to
see her only son launched into the very top of the
tonnish world, and to this end she exhausted what
fortune she had in providing Alex with the very
best schools, horses, clothes, and other accouter-
ments of the fashionable life. When he had a fancy
to join the army, she had bought him a lieutenancy.
And when, after a taste of battle in the hard Spanish campaign, he had decided the military was not
for him, she had haunted the Horse Guards to
plead his cause. She supported his hunters and his
hacks and his phaeton, for Alex had sulkily
informed her that no gentleman could live without
these equine accessories. She had paid his gaming
debts without complaint and encouraged him to
patronize Stultz & Weston, two of the city's most
fashionable tailors, where he had run up such
enormous bills that she had to rescue him from a
sponging house. More than once, she had paid for
his follies with the Cyprians of the Metropolis.
When she finally died, she was at least happy in
the belief that her boy was at the top of the fashionable world. But with her death, her jointure
was at an end.

The small fortune Alex inherited would have
been sufficient to allow him to live comfortably,
perhaps even luxuriously, had he learned habits of
economy. But Alex had never studied in that
school, and it was not long before he had dissipated
the entire amount, and at present his creditors
were once again pressing him for payment. Having

had one taste of life in a sponging house, he was determined not to repeat the experience.

Unlike other men of birth without the means to support themselves at some respectable occupation such as the law, the clergy, the military, or the diplomatic corps, Alex believed that the world owed him a living. He was, after all, a gentleman, and work was beneath his station in life. Having been taught this since birth, it is not surprising that the idea of work never entered his handsome head.

Instead, Alex had examined his skills and decided that gaming was his forte. Therefore, he turned his hand to making a living at cards. When he had first encountered Sally Blythe at Almack's, he had been doing pretty well. At least well enough to keep up his pretensions to the fashionable life of the Upper Ten Thousand. No one knew that cards were his sole source of income. After all, no gentleman made a living as a Captain Sharp! Just about the same time that Great Aunt Sarah had died in Bath, Alex had decided that it was time to rusticate for a time. At least until the rumors about his honesty at cards died down.

When he encountered Mrs. Bedford at Tunbridge Wells, he pegged her as a sharp at once, and she him when they caught each other cheating at a friendly game of whist in the Assembly Rooms, both of them intent on fleecing the same pigeons. Like Alex, Mrs. Bedford, an improvident widow, lived a precariously fashionable life, teetering always on the edge of ruin in an attempt to support an extravagant life. Since she had a great desire to try her luck in the Metropolis, and Alex, town-bred, was never happy outside of Mayfair, theirs was an interesting alliance.

With Alex to steer ripe pigeons like Julia to Half Moon Street, ready to be plucked by Mrs. Bedford and her friends, the discreet little establishment had prospered through the Season. It had even become quite the fashionable place to be seen and to see some of the more dashing members of the ton as they whiled away their evenings at games of chance beneath the hard-glittering smile of dear Mrs. Bedford. And of course, for every pigeon plucked, Alex has received his commission.

How did he rationalize this most dishonest behavior with his self-portrait as the complete gentleman? Very simply; the fashionable world owed him a living. People like Lady Tilghman had far too much money and too little common sense. If they would not tell fuzzed cards and shaved dice, so much the worse for them!

Now, of course, the Season was drawing to its close. Mrs. Bedford, wise enough to understand the whims of fashion would make her house quite passé by the following spring, was planning a trip to the Continent. Paris and the Palais Royal beckoned her, and she was of a mind to keep a step before the Bow Street Runners.

As usual, Alex had been improvident. Ill-gotten gains that should have gone to satisfy his tailors, his vintners, his clubs, his livery stable, and a host of other creditors whose demands were steadily growing less polite, had slipped through his hands

on a series of interesting vices, many of these
involving females both respectable and shady.

For, as it has been noted, females were attracted
to Alex Quartermaine in much the same way that
felines are attracted to catnip. Perhaps he felt no
guilt in leading Julia into five thousand pounds of
debt because she had done him the insult of being
faithful to her husband rather than succumbing to
his lures. She was one of the few to do so!

If Alex had a heart, it would have been a surprise to most of the females who had dealt with
him in the past. There was nothing he enjoyed
more than flirting, which he accomplished with a
vengeance, first making one female then another
the object of his intense attentions. Just when the
lady thought he was hers, off Alex would fly to the
next victim, leaving the first lady demolished. Sally
had been the object of his intense attentions when
she had been forced to quit the Season. The
moment Mrs. Blythe and her daughters had retreated
to Oxfordshire for the funeral, Alex had forgotten
about Sally as completely as if she had never existed.
If he had the faintest hint that she had clung to her
hopes concerning him over the past year, he would
have been amused. It was only by the sheerest
chance that he had encountered Julia and only
impelled by fashion that he had become a member
of her court.

When Sally had returned to town, engaged to
Will, he had perceived a desperate deception and
had been vastly amused. It had been his plan to
fleece Julia of her money, all the while conducting a

heartbreak flirtation with Sally, leading her on until she broke it off with Will. But the discovery that she was heiress to fifty thousand pounds had made him reconsider his position.

Of late, Alex Quartermaine had begun to realize that he was neither as young nor as skilled as he had been even a year before. A dissipated life, after all, is hardly conducive to good looks or steady hands. He had no desire to try his luck as a professional gambler on the Continent, and even in his present state, he could sense that there could come a time when not even the kindest Patroness of Almack's could ignore the rumors about his gambling habits. The hideous fate of Brummell was fresh in his mind, too. Not for him the shabby exile in Calais!

Accordingly, he had begun to think that marrying a rich wife would be a very good thing. Unfortunately, there were very few heiresses on the market at that time, and those who knew him, like Miss Margaret Mercer Elphinstone, were far too well aware of his reputation as a heartless flirt to give him much consideration, while the rich Cit's daughters were more interested in acquiring a title than a handsome commoner, no matter how tonnish. There was *one* wealthy and titled lady he knew, quite well, who might consider marriage with him, but she, he thought with a little shudder, would keep him on short shrift, for she was his match in every way. And perhaps the one thing Alex Quartermaine feared was a female who was his match in every way.

Now, the creditors grew more pressing and less

polite, so that not even ordering a new suit of
clothes or a fresh hunter worked to keep them at
bay. And it looked as if Mrs. Bedford was about to
fold her tent and steal into the night. Sally and her
fifty thousand pounds did not look quite so
unattractive. She was, it is true, not the great beauty
Julia was, but she was not unhandsome, either, and
she was devoted to him. And there was no way her
parents or Julia and Tilghman would ever allow her
to starve once the fifty thousand pounds were
gone. Although, of course, he might be gone once
the money was gone.

Alexander Quartermaine smiled to himself and
snapped his fingers, summoning a waiter to come
and replenish his glass. Satisfied, he leaned back in
his club chair, spreading his fingers. Slowly he
brought his hands together until his fingertips
touched, then smiled as he considered the best way
to pursue his quarry.

"Well, I am sure that you are entitled to your
opinion," Julia said to Sally. "And perhaps I was
wrong. Come, my dear, let us not quarrel over the
matter."

Sally looped her arm around her sister's waist.
"You know that I don't want to come to cross-crabs
with you," she said. "I am simply glad that you and
Tilghman are getting along better now."

"Well, yes, I am very glad of that, too! And that
is why I think we should not argue. Perhaps I was a
little harsh in judging Alex."

Sally smiled, but inwardly, she wished that Julia would argue with her a little, if only so that she could confirm her own opinions of Alex and put to rest the whispering doubts she could not quite suppress.

It had been a week since she had last seen Will, a week that had passed without so much as a word from him.

At first she had firmly told herself that she cared not a whit whether she ever saw him again, and thrown herself into the London whirl with a fierce, almost reckless abandon. In this she was ably assisted by Alex, who escorted her everywhere, pressing her, indeed almost overwhelming her with his attentions. It was Alex at the ball, Alex at Almack's, Alex at the rout parties, the Royal Academy Show at Somerset House, Alex at the balloon ascension on the Thames, Alex in the park. In short, if Miss Blythe was there, she was sure to have the escort of Mr. Quartermaine. Never had he exerted himself to be more charming or attentive!

She had only to express a fondness for violets to have bouquets of the flower descend upon Tilghman House as if it were spring and not autumn. If she said she liked Hayden, Alex was there with tickets to the concert in the park. It had been seven straight days of Alex, and if Sally were to be quite honest with herself, which she was decidedly not, she would have admitted that his company in such intense doses was a little wearing. How had she never noticed that in his company, the conversation could start anywhere, but always seemed to devolve back to the subject of Alex? His interests were not with current events, or books or music, but passionately centered on the style of the moment. The opinions of the trendsetters were his opinions. He treated those he considered his inferiors with contempt while fawning upon those he considered his social superiors, with the result that she often found him to be a bit of a toadeater and a bully.

Church services saw him not, and he was a stranger to the lending libraries. She was growing increasingly uneasy with the manner in which he handled his horses and treated his servants. Why had she never noticed that he was unable to pass a mirror without glancing into its depths at his own reflection?

In short, he was beginning to irritate her. So, being Sally, and being unable to admit, even to herself that she was wrong, she clung to him, defending him against all criticism.

"I can't understand what you see in the fellow! Why would you let a perfectly fine man like Will Starret go for that Bond Street Beau?" Tilghman asked bluntly when news that she had cried off her engagement was presented to him.

Since Sally's response had been to quit the room in tears, leaving her brother-in-law to turn to his wife and demand, in all masculine innocence, what the devil he had said.

"Oh, my dear, it's the talk of the town," Julia said. "You know how people will talk when a couple cries off. We're just fortunate that no one sent announcements to the papers."

"Yes, I suppose so," Tilghman replied doubtfully.

"Never made any secret of the fact that I don't much like Quartermaine, though. Reeks of scent."

If it was in the tip of Julia's tongue to make some remark about Lady Rockhall, she held her peace. The hope, however vague, that she might soon be out of her difficulties had made her more cheerful.

This afternoon, Alex having made an engagement to meet with them there, Julia was able to persuade her sister to bear her company for a drive through the park. "For you look just a little peaked, you know, and the fresh air will do you good," Julia had said.

The picture the Blythe sisters made being driven in her ladyship's crested barouche was charming. Julia wore a sarcenet carriage dress of a light geranium color and a Pamela hat of royal purple velvet with a rouleau of gold satin, while Sally wore a Levantine silk pelisse of lilac and a British leghorn bonnet edged in blue satin. Against the chill of late afternoon, she carried a Norwich shawl.

"I can't help but feel as if everyone is looking at us and gossiping," she said uneasily to Julia, who was busy smiling and nodding at all their acquaintance and enjoying herself hugely.

"Oh, your broken engagement is quite passé," Julia replied lightly, waving and smiling at Lady Holland. "The *new* on-dit is Miss Haverstraw."

"Miss Haverstraw?" Sally repeated. "Who is Miss Haverstraw?"

"Oh, you've been spending so much time with Alex you're quite out of things," Julia replied. "She is just come to town from Dublin. A great beauty.

In fact, she puts me quite in the shade," she remarked naively. "And a great heiress, too. She'll have all of old Lord Fishguard's fortune, they say."

At that moment a familiar phaeton hove into view, with Will at the reins and a lovely blonde, all in celestial blue seated up beside him. "That is Miss Haverstraw!" Julia breathed. "Isn't she lovely? At least Will seems to think so!"

At the sight of Will, looking so handsome in his blue Bath superfine jacket and buckskins, Sally's heart gave an unexpected start. As she was about to raise her hand in greeting, she had a good look at Miss Haverstraw, and her heart sank again.

Perhaps it was the way in which Will was talking to her, their heads so close together, her small hand, gloved in York tan, resting for a moment on his arm. He looked so happy. Happier, Sally thought, with a stab of jealousy, than he had ever looked with her!

As the two vehicles drew abreast, Will, as if barely able to take his attention from Miss Haverstraw's charms, turned slowly in their direction. "Hullo, Julia, Sally!" he said. "Caroline, I'd like you to meet two friends of mine."

Friends. Sally barely heard the introductions being made. The word *friend* seemed to have stopped her thoughts. And when she had a full glimpse of the lovely Miss Haverstraw, it was all she could do to smile politely and extend her hand.

And yet, there was something about the Irish heiress that looked familiar, although she could not place it. "Have we met before?" she asked.

Miss Haverstraw's blue eyes, deeply fringed with dark lashes, closed for a moment, lying on her creamy skin. "No, I don't think so," she said in a clear, lilting voice. "I certainly would have recalled you, Miss Blythe. Have you ever been to Dublin?"

Will grinned as if he were stunned, Sally noted with distaste. Obviously, he was deeply infatuated with Miss Haverstraw, Sally thought, and who could blame him? She was the most beautiful creature Sally had ever seen. Hair the color of newly minted guineas curled becomingly from beneath a celestial bonnet trimmed with Brussels lace. Dark lashes, blue eyes, creamy skin, all perfection. There was no blemish to mar that pure complexion, no unsightly crook to that perfect little nose. Her lips were red and luscious and the figure Sally could see beneath the sky-blue kerseymere pelisse was about as perfect as it was possible for the female form to be. No wonder Will looked so pleased and happy with himself. He had certainly not let any grass grow beneath his feet, she thought resentfully.

Yes, Miss Haverstraw had been vouchered for Almack's, she was telling Julia in that low, musical voice. And Mr. Starret had been so kind as to promise provide her his escort there this Tuesday next.

Hearing this, Sally almost gasped. Will, who had made her promise that she would never ask him to go to Almack's was now escorting Miss Haverstraw there! Something very much like resentment stirred in her and it was all that she could do to keep her smile rigidly plastered on her face.

Mr. Starret, whom she had met through her cousin, Barney Tennant, had been so very kind to her, taking her to all the fashionable amusements, Miss Haverstraw said. "Why, tonight, he's promised to take me to Vauxhall Gardens!"

Sally's fingers twisted around the handle of her parasol. But she kept on smiling until it felt as if her jaw would ache for a week after. She was so intent upon Miss Haverstraw and Will that she did not even notice when Alex Quartermaine rode up on his bay hack.

Miss Haverstraw noticed Mr. Quartermaine, however, and swept him with an appreciative look, blushing becomingly as Will introduced him. And it was certain that Alex noted Miss Haverstraw. Someone might have lit a candle behind his eyes.

Nothing could have been more calculated to charm than the way in which Alex took her small gloved hand in his own and brushed his lips against the air above it, nor the compliment he paid her on her bonnet. "How do you do?" he asked, and made those simple words sound like an invitation to much more intimate things.

Miss Haverstraw, with all the appearance of one surrendering to enchantment, beamed prettily. "Not *the* Mr. Quartermaine!" she exclaimed, twirling the ribbons of her bonnet. "Why we've heard of you, even in Dublin!"

Alex looked gratified, and would have pursued this line, if Will had not been frowning at him so severely.

"We really ought to be on our way," Will said

after a glance at his watch. "Your chaperone will be wondering where we are."

"You know, perhaps we should accept Lady Tilghman's very civil offer to chaperone us to Vauxhall," Miss Haverstraw said to Will, laying her hand again on his sleeve. "My aunt finds Vauxhall so fatiguing, Mr. Starret."

"I say, Jules, you are a friend!" Will exclaimed. "Would you?"

"I would be delighted!" Julia replied. "I haven't been to Vauxhall all Season! Now that town is becoming so thin to company, it would be the perfect antidote to boredom."

Sally, who had not heard this offer being made, looked at her sister suspiciously. Julia merely smiled. "I find myself free on Thursday. Would that suit?"

After some conversation, it was decided that it would. "I'd ask you if you wanted to come, Sally, but I know you are engaged to go to Lady Abercorne's that night," her sister said.

Will patted Miss Haverstraw's hand. "You'll enjoy it immensely. It's all the go!" he promised.

Miss Haverstraw said she very much looked forward to it, bid Julia good day, smiled upon Sally and threw a long, backward glance at Alex as Will's phaeton pulled away.

"Now, who is Miss Haverstraw?" Alex asked as soon as they were out of earshot, his eyes still following the blue bonnet as it disappeared down the pathway.

Julia laughed. "Don't you know? And I thought you were up to every rig and row in town, Alex!

She's old Fishguard's heiress! Pots and pots of lovely Dublin guineas there, you know! Apparently, she's an orphan, been in some school there. She's out in Dublin, but apparently she hasn't been fired off in London quite yet, from what she said. I daresay she'll cause a stir!"

"Yes! I daresay!" Alex repeated distantly. A muscle in his jaw worked.

Julia continued in her gossipy way, "Apparently, she loves to play cards. That's what they do in Dublin, I suppose. Perhaps it's all the crack over there! She was telling me that she was hoping to receive a card of invitation to one of Mrs. Bedford's little parties."

Alex looked very thoughtful, and Julia examined the strings of her reticule with great interest before giving the coachman the signal to continue on.

Sally looked down at her parasol and was surprised to see that she had shredded all the ribbons on the handle. She was so involved with her own thoughts that she didn't note Alex still standing in the path gazing at the retreating blue bonnet as Will's phaeton smartly turned the corner and moved out of view.

It took him several moments to dig in his spurs and impel his horse catch up with the barouche. Like Sally, he seemed lost in his own thoughts, not even seeing Princess Lieven as she waved to them in passing.

"That reminds me," Alex finally said to Sally, leaning into the carriage. "I have discovered that a cousin of mine is coming to town on Thursday.

There's really no way I can hope to avoid seeing her. She's quite elderly and lives in Bath most of the time. She's coming to see her doctor. You understand how it is! I hope you will forgive me if I beg off the Abercornes with you?"

"Of course," Sally said indifferently, her thoughts going in quite another direction. Alex might not have even been there as far as she was concerned. "I quite understand how it is."

A look of relief passed over his face. "Well, I'm glad that's settled! I'll make it up to you, Sally, I promise. But now I've really go to be going. I just recalled an appointment with my tailor."

Sally merely nodded. She did not see Alex rein about and start off at a brisk trot down the path in the direction Will and Miss Haverstraw had taken.

"Do you think Will is falling in love with her?" she asked her sister. Although she tried to keep her tone indifferent, there was a thread of doubt in her voice.

Julia smiled beneath the brim of her hat.

Sally was still too distracted to notice when Julia announced, as they returned to Tilghman House, that it had been a most productive afternoon.

Julia was not surprised when Sally came into her dressing room on Thursday saying that she had changed her mind and would like to go to Vauxhall Gardens with her. Julia, who was seated at her dressing table with Pomfret dressing her hair, exchanged a look with her abigail.

"That would be very nice," she replied evenly.
"We would be very glad to have you, Sally, if you
want to come with us. But I thought you were set
on going to the Abercornes?"

"The Abercorne's parties are dead bores and
Angela Abercorne's a dowdy quiz," Sally said sullenly, leaning against the ornate screen in the corner and focusing her attention on her toes. "All she
can talk about is seeing Will everywhere with Miss
Haverstraw."

"Oh?" Julia asked.

"I've changed my mind," Sally said defensively.
"I can do that, can't I?"

"I suppose you can. But you said—"

"It is always a female's prerogative to change her
mind," Sally sulked.

"Of course you are welcome! I didn't mean that
you weren't. It is just that—"

"What? You can't possibly think I'm mooning
over Will, can you?"

"Oh, dear no! I am sure that you are correct, and
that Alex is a much better choice for you, Sally!
Speaking of Alex, I haven't seen him very much
these past few days."

"His cousin is visiting," Sally replied.

"Oh, yes, his cousin."

Tilghman suddenly appeared in the doorway.
"Going out again tonight?" he asked.

"Pomfret," Julia said, "Why don't you take Miss
Julia and look in the cedar closet for that pomona
green shawl I bought last spring? It would look very
becomingly with your jonquil sarcenet tonight, Sally."

As soon as they had left the room, she turned and looked at her husband. "Vauxhall Gardens. I know, I know, it's shockingly vulgar, but it should be interesting. Are you going to the House?"

"Late session, unfortunately!" he replied with a grimace. "We've got to get this bill passed."

"Tilghman, do you notice anything different?" Julia asked.

Her husband promptly took on the expression of a man who has been asked by his wife if he notices something has changed.

"That's a very becoming hairstyle," he said hopefully.

"No, but thank you! No more workmen! Tilghman, the house is finished! The draper put up the curtains in the Gold Reception Room this afternoon."

Tilghman looked around as if he expected a stray upholsterer or painter to wander down the hall. "Done?" he repeated.

"Done!" Julia repeated triumphantly. "Now I can really start being a help to you in your career! Just as soon as I get rid of Alex . . . and . . . and take care of some other things, we can be comfortable again!"

"But—" he broke off, surrendering to female logic. Something was afoot, but he did not know what, and what was more, recognized that he was probably better of in his ignorance. He hoped that it had something to do with expunging Alex Quartermaine from his household forever, but was not sanguine on this point as he took himself away to change into his evening clothes.